Post Card

PLACE STAMP HERE
DOMESTIC ONE CENT
FOREIGN TWO CENTS

The Adventures of a Common Man

FOR ADDRESS ONLY

POST CARD

PLACE STAMP HERE
DOMESTIC ONE CENT
FOREIGN TWO CENTS

The Adventures of a Common Man

Edmond P. DeRousse

FOR ADDRESS ONLY

Tate Publishing & *Enterprises*

The Adventures of a Common Man
Copyright © 2009 by Edmond P. DeRousse. All rights reserved.

No part of this publication may be reproduced, stored in a retrieval system or transmitted in any way by any means, electronic, mechanical, photocopy, recording or otherwise without the prior permission of the author except as provided by USA copyright law.

This novel is a work of fiction. However, several names, descriptions, entities, and incidents included in the story are based on the lives of real people.

The opinions expressed by the author are not necessarily those of Tate Publishing, LLC.

Published by Tate Publishing & Enterprises, LLC
127 E. Trade Center Terrace | Mustang, Oklahoma 73064 USA
1.888.361.9473 | www.tatepublishing.com

Tate Publishing is committed to excellence in the publishing industry. The company reflects the philosophy established by the founders, based on Psalm 68:11,
"The Lord gave the word and great was the company of those who published it."

Book design copyright © 2009 by Tate Publishing, LLC. All rights reserved.
Cover design by Tyler Evans
Interior design by Joey Garrett

Published in the United States of America

ISBN: 978-1-61566-321-7
1. Fiction / Humorous
2. Fiction / Biographical
09.10.12

Table of Contents

INTRODUCTION	9
PREFACE	13
FAMILY HISTORY	19
SUMMERVILLE WOODS	27
THE OL' COLLEGE TRY	37
NUTS	45
THE ARMY PHYSICAL	49
KING SHANNON (OR WHEN I DISCOVERED DOGS TALK)	57
FIRSTBORN	65
FISHING ON THE REBEDEOUX	71
NEIGHBORLY LOVE	81
THE END OF AN ERA	89
CIVILIAN AGAIN	101
TIGHT PANTS	109

ZPG	117
MURPHY'S ARMY	125
THE IDOC PHYSICAL	137
THE SPANISH INVASION	145
THE INTERVENTION (HOW GOD IS DEALING WITH ME)	163
MURDER IN MY CLASSROOM	173
A DATE WITH BRIANNA	179
THE RACING ZEBRA	187
THE LITTLE ZEBRA	195
THE ADULT WAY	201
LOST	211
MINI ADVENTURES	219
EPILOGUE (A LOVE STORY)	225

Introduction

This is the story of Pete Russey. He is a sixty-year-old man who has been married nearly forty years to the same woman. He has had a full life. Pete is not a handsome man, but neither is he unattractive. Like most of us he has had missed opportunities and been smart enough to take advantage of others. He was born in the early fifties in the era of black and white TVs, am radios, and .28 cents per gallon gasoline. Times were simple and uncomplicated.

The social values were much different when Pete was born. Family stability was extremely important. Men and women stayed married no matter what the difficulty. Keeping oneself working is how the family stayed together.

Pete's dad was the undisputed head of the house. He taught his children that the job was the only important value. Hard work and loyalty would always make life rewarding. Living up to those expectations presented Pete with constant challenges. Because employment was the only important value, Pete was never long without it, and that afforded him the opportunity to experience much.

Pete was the fourth of five kids. He feels there were advantages and disadvantages to his placement in the Russey family. It was easy to get lost in the crowd when blame had to be passed around. It also made it difficult to be noticed when everyone had needs at the same time.

Being one of five children makes learning to be

adventurous a necessity. Each sibling developed his or her own distinct personality. The oldest and youngest, both girls, were very outgoing and quite freethinking. The middle two, one boy and one girl, were the quiet ones and probably because of that always seemed to get extra support from their parents.

Pete, the fourth in line, was not first, last, or in the middle. Finding his way in the family unit was difficult. He learned early in his life how to not be the ignored one.

Pete was constantly striving to gain the favor of his father. Perhaps that explains why he explored so many careers.

Pete did not acknowledge the existence of God until late in his life. When he did, his life changed, causing him to reevaluate the value system he was taught in his youth.

The combination of simple, uncomplicated times, his instilled family values, and his constant striving for his father's respect are what makes this common man what he is.

These are his adventures.

Preface

My name is Pierre Jacque Russey. My friends call me Pete. I would like to invite you into my world. If you take up my offer and enter, be forewarned. You just might find yourself identifying with it.

I am not a famous personality. I have not done anything to draw extraordinary attention to myself. I haven't even had my fifteen minutes of fame yet. (Although, hopefully, with this book I will achieve that.) I am just a common, everyday, ordinary man.

My wife, CJ, and I have been married over thirty-five years. We have two grown children and two grandchildren. The grandchildren were an absolute surprise. Our children have been out of our home and living on their own for several years. They were so focused on their own lives that we told all our friends we were content just to have grandpuppies. Our daughter has two boxers, hence our grandpuppies. But life is funny and full of the unexpected. They each blessed us with a grandson.

I have been teaching in a state correctional facility for nearly eighteen years. CJ is a substitute teacher and employed by several schools in several counties. We are both members of a local Lutheran church.

We met as blind dates and later became high school sweethearts. She is the first and only girl I ever kissed. We graduated from the same college. Neither of us have been on television, in a movie, or mentioned in a newspaper article. I did write a letter to the editor a couple of times and once even had my hand on TV.

CJ and I work hard, pay our bills, enjoy our family, and go to church on Sundays. We have no fancy-sounding job titles. The home is small. So is the SUV. Heck, we are ordinary folk.

So why am I writing this book? It's more of a journal, actually. You might call this a series of therapy sessions. No, this is not a tell-all book about how he or she did this or that and I-want-you-to-feel-sorry-for-me book. I just have stories in me trying to get out. And writing them is certainly cheaper than lying on a couch and paying a doctor to listen to them.

In my nearly six decades on this planet, I have had many adventures. From 1968 to today, I have had nearly forty mailing addresses. That in itself creates the opportunity for many adventures. Unfortunately, many trees gave up their lives to make the boxes and paper we needed for all those moves.

I have been thinking about writing a book for about twenty years. I even made notes. The book was going to be about things I experienced as a youth. But I lost my notes.

I wasn't giving up on my dream, though, so about ten years ago, I decided the book would be geared toward my adult life. I made plans to write *The Autobiography of a Great Man*. It was going to be funny, sad, romantic, entertaining, and Indiana Jones adventurous. A definite bestseller. I expected Steven Spielberg to offer me millions for the privilege to make his movie version, starring me of course.

About two years ago, I realized that those adventures I imagined had not yet happened and honestly at my age were not likely to happen. I started to believe no one would be interested in an autobiography of a common man. I thought, *Who would read a self-written book about someone not in the news or not being known for doing something spectacular to change life?* Out of frustration, my dream of writing a book was put on hold once again. I still wanted to write one; I just didn't know what to write about.

A few months ago, something happened in my classroom. After telling others about it, I realized I just wrote a short story. I only had to put it on paper. It was that story that helped me decide the format for this book. My therapy sessions could now begin.

This book is not long in pages. You will not be challenged with big words. It is not intended to occupy much of your valuable time.

I gauge the book I am about to read by two very strict criteria. I do not want to have to think about what I just read, and most importantly, it cannot be thick. I have to read this book before you do, so it must comply with my criteria.

Take this book with you to the airport, to the train station, or to the doctor's office. Read it while you wait. A friend of mine uses his john time to read a copy I gave him. My children read their copy to their infant children. It may help you pass the time.

Hopefully, you will spend time in the therapy sessions of this common man and help keep his doctor bills to a minimum. I believe you will find these sessions entertaining.

If you do decide to turn the page and begin reading about my adventures, I am sure you will find something that will at least make you smile.

Enjoy!

Family History

Everyone has a family history. Funny thing about it, though, is we remember the interesting stuff. The rest we forget, deny it happened, or do not recall it the same way as others.

I have one younger sister, one older brother, and two older sisters. Between the younger sibling and me is a three-year difference in age. Between my oldest sister and me is ten years. My brother is five years older, and my middle sister is six years older.

My family lived in a large house. I didn't really pay much attention to it growing up. I just lived there. But describing it to my children years later made me realize how big it was. When they hear me describe the house, my children accuse me of being born with a silver spoon in my mouth.

The house sat up on a slight hill. I always thought it looked like it belonged in the English countryside. It had two stories and a full basement.

The downstairs had a kitchen with a pantry off to one side and a master bath on the other. It had a large dining room and a long, long table where the Russey family ate all their meals. The table had to be long to service our large family. The large living room, the size of two rooms, had a fireplace in it. I always imagined as a kid that the ceiling in the room had to be twenty feet tall. This is the room where we would put our live Christmas tree. The Christmas tree would be decorated from floor to ceiling. I especially enjoyed watching the bubble lights.

The living room was the absolute most fun room to be in within the house. We would gather around the fireplace when it was cold outside. My responsibility was to build the fire. The floors had a varnished wood flooring that provided entertainment for the children of the house. Sliding around on the floor in our shoes covered with socks was great fun. This happened every time Mom waxed the floor.

Mom and Dad's bedroom was also located on the first floor. It was later converted to the family room when Dad turned our living room into his optometric office.

The second floor was where the kids slept. I do not remember my oldest sister ever having a room in the house. She had already moved out by the time I started being aware of things. My middle sister and my youngest sister each had their own room. I shared the largest bedroom with my older brother. The upstairs also had three large walk-in closets and a bathroom. Each closet was large enough to be a small room.

I think I told my kids the house I grew up in had twenty rooms including those large upstairs closets.

The house had character. It was a shame when Mom and Dad moved and they sold it to the bank. The bank tore it down and made a parking lot out of it.

I know that each of the siblings has a different perspective of our family history. I'm sure that's because of the thirteen-year age difference between the oldest and the youngest. We each tell or remember our history differently. Knowing my father, he most likely told a different version of the same story. He may have also made up new stories for each of his five children to pass down to their children.

Some of our history can be substantiated as true or partly true. Some is most likely fabricated.

I cannot remember my mother sharing too much about her family history. She let my father do most of that. I know she had history to share because she came from a large family. Mom was the only girl in a family with four brothers. One, Harry, left a lasting impression on me.

Harry was the practical joker in my mother's family. Every time Mom or Dad talked of him, it would be about a practical joke he played on someone.

Mom's prankster brother worked in a steel mill in Johnstown, Pennsylvania. On a particularly cold winter day, Harry decided to play a joke on his boss that literally backfired. Mom's version of the story was that Harry caught his boss napping in his chair during lunch. My uncle decided to make life a little interesting for his boss. He snuck up behind the napping boss, pulled out a lighter, and held the lighter near the exposed head. According to Mom, her brother was only trying to wake up his boss before lunchtime ended.

It was not very well thought out. The boss's hair caught on fire. Believe it or not, the boss didn't wake up until Harry rolled the man out of his chair. Mom said Harry could never understand why his boss became such a hothead after that.

I later had a chance to relate that incident to Uncle

Harry. He denied it, but there was a twinkle in his eye when I spoke of it to him.

I was the recipient of one of his practical jokes when he came to visit us one summer.

Uncle Harry and Mom were talking in the kitchen when I came in to get something to eat. When he saw me, he picked up what looked like a plastic bottle with dishwashing detergent in it and started smelling it. I believed he was helping Mom wash the supper dishes. He told me the liquid smelled like chocolate cake. I didn't believe him, of course. He offered me a smell. When I put my nose to the bottle to take a sniff, he squeezed the bottle. I was sure I saw liquid squirting out, so naturally I backed off and harmlessly tripped over a kitchen chair. Harry started laughing, hysterically. All that came out of the bottle was a string. He must have been waiting for some unsuspecting person to fall prey to that joke.

My father had many stories about the Russey clan, and he relished telling them. One of the first ones I remember dealt with several thousand acres of farmland deeded to his great-grandfather by the king of France. I never clearly understood why the land was donated. Being young and easily influenced by my father, I was only impressed by the family connection to a king. Today, all I really know for sure is that I have relatives owning farmland in the general vicinity of Dad's legend. Those relatives have neither confirmed nor denied the story.

Many families who have a history of ancestors living in our American West have stories about cowboys and Indians. This is my dad's story. I don't remember much of the details. I just remember what I thought was the impressive part.

His great-grandmother, Ester, was traveling west in a wagon train with her family. They were headed to the gold fields of California. I think Dad said somewhere in western Oklahoma the wagon train was attacked by Indians on the warpath. The wagon train had stopped for the night when the attack occurred. It was just before supper, and Ester had wandered off. Just as her parents were starting to search for their misplaced child, the Indians came riding in, guns blazing.

Ester had evidently witnessed the attack and hid in the nearby bushes. I've been to Oklahoma, and I don't think there are many nearby bushes. Everyone in the wagon train was massacred.

The Indians later found Ester wandering alone. One of the warriors picked her up and presented her to the Indian chief. I don't remember the rest of the details except that somehow Ester grew up and married an Indian chief. That is how Dad could justify saying we had Indian blood in us. As a youngster, being able to say I was related to an Indian princess was impressive. Of course, this story cannot be verified. I don't know if I will pass this story along to my grandchildren with the urgency my father passed it to me. I don't think Indians, unfortunately, have the same glamour they once had.

My father and mother were both doctors of optometry. They met, fell in love, and married while in optometric school. My dad's father was one of the first licensed optometrist in the state of Illinois. Dad once showed me an optometry license with my grandfather's name on it. The number on the license definitely proved my father's claim. We are very proud of the fact that our family was part of the beginning of licensed optometry in Illinois. My father always expected one of his sons to continue that history. We could not. Life had other plans.

Dad always told me that we were one of the three oldest families in the state. He said records indicated that our family was among the first to settle on Kaskaskia Island, which is where Illinois basically began. I once did a high school English paper on the history of Kaskaskia Island. Although my research verified that our family was among the first in Illinois, I could not verify Dad's insistence that we were one of the three oldest families.

One of my favorite family history stories involved Lewis and Clarke. Dad never changed the following story. He frequently reminded me that we had a Russey on the Lewis and Clarke expedition. In fact, he said, our ancestor was the third oarsman in the Clarke boat. I proudly told that story many times throughout my youth and into my adulthood. A few years ago, I located a list of crew members of the entire expedition. There were no names on it resembling anything close to our name. It appears that one was a fairy tale I wanted to believe was true.

When I was very young, my parents shared with me how they came up with my name. Both my parents have the same strange story.

Mom and Dad were visiting Fort Kaskaskia when Mom was about eight months pregnant with me. They had not yet decided on a name for me.

Many of our ancestors are buried in the cemetery there. While reading names on tombstones, my mom and dad found a family name they liked. How many of you can tell your friends that your name came off a tombstone?

I cannot verify if this story is true. Mom and Dad both said that is where my name came from. I have, though, located the tombstone I believed they used as my namesake. It's interesting history that I intend to pass on to my children and grandchildren. Let them speculate about it.

Family history is important. It is who we were, who we are, and determines who we will become. We can learn from it and make improvements or choose to ignore it and change nothing.

What family history is passed on is left up to my children after I am gone.

Post Card

PLACE STAMP HERE
DOMESTIC ONE CENT
FOREIGN TWO CENTS

Summerville Woods

FOR ADDRESS ONLY

I grew up in a small town in southern Illinois in the 1950s and 1960s. Life was simpler then. Actually, I think Mayberry might resemble the lifestyle then. Computers, cell phones, or Xbox games were not needed to have fun. The great outdoors could provide plenty of that.

One of the summertime activities of many young men was camping. Yes, girls and cars were important. This adventure will include both those pastimes. How could any kind of a story about teenage boys not include girls and cars?

Two or three miles to the south of town was Summerville Woods. It was a haven for those of us who liked to camp. I have no idea who owned the woods. Whoever did had to know it was a frequent camping spot. We always pitched our tents in the same location every time we went to the woods. It was on top of a hill and overlooked a rock road.

These campouts would usually take place on a Friday night. Saturday was reserved for cruising around with our girlfriends. Most of us would arrive at the campsite around 4:00 to 5:00 p.m. Someone would build a campfire for cooking. It was the middle of July. I don't why we built a fire. I guess we were just pyros. Each of us brought our own supper to cook. These suppers would vary from hot dogs to marinated steaks.

In the summer of 1967, shortly after the Fourth of July, I decided to pack my tent and head out to

Summerville Woods with several of my friends. My meal on this night was carefully chosen. It had to be easy to cook. I was going to barbecue a hamburger.

This was the first time John Smith had ever been camping. He had heard about our infamous campouts. We never cared who camped with us. We only had one condition, and that was all first-time campers had to go snipe hunting with us. Snipe hunting was a ritual, and its secrets were not to be shared. John had agreed to the hunt.

Anyone who has ever been snipe hunting knows it cannot happen until it is completely dark. Snipes are nocturnal creatures. They are also extremely rare. Because of their rarity, it would be highly unlikely that John would actually catch one. John was a competitor and accustomed to winning. This was shaping up to be a really great night.

In southern Illinois in July, the dark of night would come late. My friends and I had all the equipment ready for the night's activity. In our part of the world, snipe hunting required a burlap bag, a walking stick, a rope, and the all-important snipe food.

The burlap bag was used to hold the captured snipe. The walking stick was used to chase the snipe out of its hiding place and for protection if needed. Of course, the food was used for enticement.

There have been reports of snipes attacking people. So you have to be careful how you hunt them. We told John that our group was considered by many in the community to be the experts on hunting these creatures. John knew he could trust us. He couldn't wait to get started.

About two hours after supper, someone said he thought he heard a snipe. It was time to go hunting. The group gathered up John and the equipment and headed down the hill into the woods. I stayed at the campsite. Someone had to chase the snipe back down into the woods if it stumbled into the campsite.

A half hour went by, and suddenly I heard a blood-curdling scream. The hair stood up on the back of my neck. I didn't know what happened. I had to stay put; someone might need me.

Bill and Jackson came laughing into the campsite. I was confused. Then they asked me if I still had any of my barbecue sauce left. I told them I did. Apparently they had forgotten to inform me about how they changed the hunt. The sauce was for the fake blood to use on Jackson. They decided to pretend Jackson got bit by the snipe. Thus the scream. I liked the impromptu addition. Jackson applied the sauce to his leg, and the two of them headed down the hill back into the woods.

A few minutes later, the group walked into the camp carrying Jackson. John appeared to be ghostly white. I'm sure it was a combination of the excitement of the hunt and concern for his fellow hunter. Jackson was moaning, and Bill had the burlap bag over his shoulder. Jackson was brought over to me. I had the first aid kit. I attended to Jackson's pretend wound while the rest of the group took turns patting John on the back. You see, he was a great hunter. He captured an elusive snipe. It was in the bag.

John wanted to see it, but we convinced him that

if he opened the bag at night it would wake up and escape. We all told John he had to wait until the morning light to open the bag.

What a great night. But it was just beginning.

It was probably around 11:00 p.m. now. We weren't quite ready to turn in for the night, and so we just sat around the campfire talking. We watched a car head down the road and stop at the bottom of the hill. The guy in the car got out. He was singing, or at least it sounded like it. Couldn't really understand him, and he was loud. We thought he was drunk and hoped he didn't know we were up on the hill. We thought there might be a girl in the car with him.

Suddenly, Bill walked to the edge of our campsite and started having a conversation with that guy. We all thought Bill was nuts. The more those two talked, the more evident it became Bill was talking to a drunk. We didn't like the fact that a drunk man now knew where we were. We did everything we could to make Bill stop his bantering with the drunk man. But Bill was having too much fun.

The man seemed to be getting angry with Bill. The drunk man started walking up our path. Apparently, the man was too drunk to navigate the path up the hill to our campsite. He stumbled and rolled back down the hill. I thought I saw him take something out of a bag and say something to it. Of that I can't be sure. It was getting too late. None of us were anxious to have him become part of our outing. Fortunately, it didn't matter anymore. He stumbled back into his car and slowly drove away.

If the snipe hunt didn't get us wound up, this drunken episode was sure to keep us up for a while longer, especially Bill. I don't know what got into him, but he was just about to lead us into another adventure. And it was now midnight.

Bill was so charged up by now; he took control of the rest of the night's activities. He told us the drunk's car looked like Jason Parker's car and that must have been his girlfriend with him. Bill suddenly acted concerned about Jason Parker's safety. He suggested we climb down the hill, follow the road for a while, and make sure Jason and his girlfriend didn't wind up in a ditch someplace.

We headed down the road. I reminded Bill that we didn't have our flashlights. He said we didn't need them. As long as we stayed on the road, we would be just fine. How odd. Why were we on a rescue mission without flashlights?

About a mile down the road, we came upon a car. As we got closer to the car, it appeared to be rocking. Bill told us to go into the bushes opposite the car and stay there until he called us. This was getting weird.

Jackson was with me on the side of the road and reminded me of something I had forgotten. Bill and Jason had a history. They didn't like each other. Bill was sure that Jason stole his girlfriend, Mary.

Bill now had an opportunity to find out if it was true. The car was really rocking now. Bill had managed to sneak up to the rear of the car undetected. He stayed there a few seconds. Suddenly, Jackson and I saw a flash and heard a loud bang.

None of us realized it, but Bill had a stash of firecrackers, and he discharged one at the rear end of that car. Whoever was in that car must have been scared to death. Bill ran across the road and told us to not move a muscle until that car left.

Bill told us that Jason was indeed parking with Mary. Jason was the school bully. And Bill just threw a lit firecracker at him.

After what seemed like minutes, Jason Parker opened the car door and headed across the road toward us. He had a club in his hand, and he was naked as a jaybird. You bet I stayed still. He was beating the ground with that club. We must have done a good job hiding because no one got clobbered with that bat.

I was pretty sure Jason threw something, and it landed near me. He got back in his car. It was a few more minutes before he drove away. Now we were absolutely convinced we had a problem. That was the school bully, and he knew where we were camping. He had friends and wasn't afraid to use them.

We headed back to camp to prepare for our slaughter.

Obviously, we weren't in a great big hurry to accommodate the school bully and his friends, so we took our time. We also knew we didn't want to get surprised out on the road. This was a dilemma. It definitely required strategy.

Lots of ideas were emerging as we made headway back to the campsite. We were so engrossed in developing plans that we almost didn't see the light coming toward us.

At first, we weren't sure what we were seeing. Bill told us to stop for a minute. Yep! It was a pair of headlights.

Oh no! It looked like two or three pairs of headlights. We needed to get out of sight in a hurry. We ran into the open field adjacent to the road and hunkered down. When the cars safely passed, we got back on the road and continued our journey to slaughter.

A few yards down the road, we heard something in the woods. What now? I didn't know how much more excitement I could take.

The night was pitch black. We all hunkered down to listen. We certainly were caught in a bad spot. The open field was on one side of us, and the woods were on the other.

Whatever we heard in the woods sounded human. We weren't about to move until we knew what we were up against.

We heard footsteps cross the road a few feet in front of us and walk into the open field. Maybe it would leave us alone. But it didn't.

That thing just kept walking up and down the field parallel to us. It was really late. Possibly early morning now. We were too tired to be scared.

Bill finally came up with a brilliant idea. He decided he would slither up a few feet, stand up, and yell. When that thing came out to attack him, the rest of us would jump on the attacker and beat it off. Sounded like a good plan to us, especially since Bill volunteered to be the attackee.

The plan worked like a charm. Bill stepped forward and screamed like a banshee. We were ready and primed. But nothing happened. Nothing came out of the field to attack us. We waited for a sneak attack. Still nothing happened. The footsteps ceased.

We all heard those footsteps walk through the woods, cross the road a few steps ahead of us, and walk up and down that open field. We never saw anything, but we all heard *something*.

I cannot for certainty say ghosts do exist, but I cannot for certainty say they do not exist either. To this day, I can still occasionally hear those footsteps. I never did find out what it was. I have heard some speculation but nothing tangible.

We finally made it back to our campsite. We totally expected company. The place was deserted, and nothing was disturbed.

It took us a while to regain our composure. Once we did, we went to sleep, woke up in the morning sunshine, fixed our breakfast, packed our gear, and left for home.

By the way, I never heard from Jason Parker. I am not convinced he was the man in Summerville Woods that night.

John finally did open up his burlap bag to see his prized snipe. After the night we just experienced, he wasn't a bit surprised to find a log in the bag.

It was a most enjoyable night indeed. And one I will never forget.

The Ol' College Try

My enrollment in college happened because I had no choice. My parents both graduated from college. My two older sisters and my older brother graduated from college. It mattered not whether I thought I was capable of handling the academics. I was not to break the family tradition.

Believe me, I was greatly concerned about my collegiate aptitude. I struggled through high school. If I had trouble getting through high school, I was sure going to have a tough time in college. I would have to try so that Mom and Dad couldn't accuse me of breaking tradition. If I failed, at least I gave it the "the ol' college try." That would be worth something.

Even though I was filled with self-doubt, I knew I would have to end up in a career my dad respected. I enjoyed and was pretty good at English. Why not be an English teacher? I respected my dad's occupation. He was an optometrist. Why not aspire to follow in his footsteps? In my youth, I enjoyed being a Boy Scout. I got involved in many service-oriented projects through scouting.

Those influences in my life would determine my career goals. My first goal was to become an optometrist. Science would be a priority. I didn't like science. But Dad would be extremely proud if I could pull that off.

I had to be realistic, though, in determining my career. A much better idea would be to become an

English teacher. I understood English. I could first get my teaching credentials and then work toward becoming an optometrist. If I didn't make it through optometry college, having a teaching certificate would give something to fall back on. Both were service oriented. I knew providing service to others was a need for me. Those were lofty goals for someone as insecure as me.

I attended Southern Illinois University in Carbondale in the late 1960s and early 1970s. The first two years were a struggle. Not being the most brilliant of students, I would spend alternate semesters on and off academic probation. Although SIU was at the time known as a party school, I was not a partygoer. I spent a great deal of time studying, but that does not ensure good grades.

I knew college students who spent more time doing drugs, drinking beer, and partying than studying. Most of them had better grades than I did. I refused to get involved in what I considered the seedy side of college life.

I survived the college academics, graduated with a degree in education, and was ready to teach.

Sometimes life has other ideas.

I got the call that many men my age dreaded. Immediately upon graduation, I was to go into the service. Optometry and teaching would be put on hold for a while.

It's been forty-five years since I set those goals. It took me thirty years before I finally became a teacher at age forty-two. Now, at age fifty-eight, I guess it's not likely I'll follow in my dad's footsteps. I have no complaints. For me, life took a good turn.

One day when I was reminiscing about my early years, I remembered a short story I wrote when I was a college freshman. For some strange reason, I kept that story. I found it (the original handwritten document) while looking through forty-year-old college pictures. That story was apparently important to me since I hid it away so I would discover it four decades later.

I have reread the story, and it definitely demonstrates how insecure I really was back then. I've come a long way since then.

My short story was written from the perspective of a college freshman in 1968 America who came from the sheltered world of a small southern Illinois town. The town and Mayberry, South Carolina, had much in common. Sheriff Andy and his son, Opy, could be walking the streets. In fact, many times I was told I looked like Opy.

I was deeply entrenched, back then, in a belief system that proposed you are your own God. This story reflects both the values of a small town and the misguided spiritual beliefs of my youth.

When the story was written, it was meant to be a serious piece of literature. Somehow I even worked in a reference to a much-revered philosopher of the day, John Lennon.

I had asked my instructor to review it. Teacher comments were written on it with the additional note, "Go ahead and type." Forty years later, I finally did.

You are about to read it. Oh! By the way, this story was not drug induced.

The Cold

As Billy sat at his desk over his homework, he thought about the conversation he had with his friend yesterday. He remembered how he thought his friend was touched. Then he recalled the content of the conversation with his friend Horace.

"It's true," said Horace.

"You're crazy. Can you prove what you just said?' retorted Billy, greatly upset.

"I don't have to. If you stop and take some time to think about it, you can come to no other conclusion."

"All right then. Let's say that illness is in the mind. How do you explain cancer? Is that also in a person's mind?" asks Billy, thinking that he finally had asked a question that would prove his buddy wrong.

"Sure it is," said Horace. "The reason a person gets cancer is because of the environment he lives in. The environment intimates that if you smoke, there is a good chance that you'll get cancer. Therefore, a man is indoctrinated with this idea and allows himself to think subconsciously that he has a chance to get this disease. That's all it takes. As soon as he admits that he has that chance, he becomes susceptible to the disease even though consciously he says he won't get it."

Billy sat in thought for a while before he made another comment. "Then what you're saying is that a man can tell himself that he won't get cancer, right?"

"That's correct. By positive thinking, a man's capabilities are infinite."

"You mean that with a positive thought, I can tell myself I'm a genius and a short time later, be one?" Billy asked his friend this question only because he wanted to continue the pretense of interest.

"Yes, but there is more to it that that. You not only have to think positive, but you also have to be confident of your capabilities. It's not enough to say that you are a genius; you have to sincerely believe that's what you are."

Billy, confused now, said, "You still haven't made yourself clear to me. Explain your theory of positive thinking."

Horace answered, "Positive thinking allows a man to do whatever he wants to do. In other words, if a man becomes afflicted with a disease such as cancer, he can cure himself because in reality he just imagines that he has it. He can heal himself by admitting that he does not have cancer and then sincerely know he does not have it. It's like a headache. Haven't you noticed that when you're active, you forget about the pain until you settle down again?"

"Yes, I've noticed that a few times."

"Forgetting about a headache is a simple thing. Anyone can do that. But to overcome a major disease such as cancer takes quite a bit of conviction. Few people have sufficient confidence to use their positive thinking in this manner. That's where I differ from most people."

Billy was stunned by his friend's confession. "Oh, so now you're saying that since you have so much confidence in yourself and believe that you can cure any disease you might develop, you think you're superior to everyone."

"Right, but I not only believe I can heal myself of disease; I know I can. And another thing: I know that I won't become afflicted with disease because I know disease does not exist. It's all in the mind. If this gives you the impression I think I'm superior to others, you're wrong. I'm superior only to those who are not confident in their power of their own positive thought."

"So you think you're Superman?"

"No. Anyone can be like me when he knows himself."

By now the conversation was beginning to make Billy wonder about his friend's sanity. Billy wondered how his friend viewed the future, so he asked, "If every person becomes confident about his positive thinking, what do you think the world in the future will be like? Judging from your remarks, it sounds as if you're saying the world will be a utopia."

"I'm no prophet, but if you are asking me for my predictions, I can give you one."

"I am."

Horace was silent for a minute before he replied. "I believe the world will live in peace. There would be no sickness, no misunderstandings, no wars, no—"

"Hang on a minute," interrupted Billy. "If everyone is thinking positive, they'll think only for themselves. There may be no illness, but I doubt seriously if there will be no misunderstandings. How do you explain that?"

"That's easy. All you have to do is educate people to think only good, positive thoughts that harm nothing."

A little upset, Billy put forth his next question. "How are you going to educate people to think good?"

"By teaching them at school. Or better yet, start teaching them as soon as they are able to learn."

Billy was now full of both wonder and anger. "I find you rather hard to believe."

"I thought you would," replied Horace.

Billy's daydream was interrupted by the ringing of the telephone. When he answered it, he heard his friend's voice.

Horace asked, "Did the math professor give us an assignment for tomorrow?"

"Yes," said Billy

"What is it?"

Billy proceeded to tell Horace the assignment. When he finished, he couldn't refrain from asking his friend why he wasn't in class that day.

"Oh, I caught a bad cold. So I went to the health service and they advised me to stay home."

I am surprised the instructor didn't tell me my story was crap.

Today, the story seems hilarious. Maturity sure changes one's perspective.

Oh well! At least I gave it the ol' college try.

Post Card

PLACE
STAMP HER
DOMESTIC
ONE CENT
FOREIGN
TWO CENTS

Nuts

FOR ADDRESS ONLY

All of us have those little adventures we wish were forgettable. They are rather humbling, actually, and others around you won't let you forget them. Here is one adventure that just won't go away.

My wife and I met through mutual friends in our senior year of high school. We lived in different communities. She lived ten miles away.

Back then most kids didn't have to travel more than fifteen or twenty miles from home for entertainment. Southern Illinois, where we lived, seemed to us to be a pretty large area. Unlike today, fifteen miles was a long way to drive, which is why I only saw my girlfriend once a week.

My little town was the place to be. It had a theater (open Thursday through Sunday), a couple of eating establishments catering to kids, and a dance hall with a variety of live bands every Saturday night. We had no need to go elsewhere.

Until college, I very seldom went beyond twenty miles from home. When I did, it was with family. The world beyond was a world I was a little afraid of venturing into. Guess I led a rather sheltered life.

That all changed with entrance into college life. My world got bigger. College was sixty miles away, and I moved there. I was mixed with all kinds of people, with all kinds of attitudes, from all over the globe. CJ entered this world with me one semester later. We would face the new world together.

CJ seemed to adapt to the changes easier than I did. CJ is one of those people who has an outgoing personality. She enjoys being around others. No one is a stranger to her. Perhaps that is why entering the college world was not difficult for her.

On Saturdays, CJ and I would frequently head to our favorite pizza palace around midafternoon and order a large pizza. For some reason, the day felt different. We were right. It started after we finished our first pizza.

Ordinarily, we would leave and head back to the college. But we were still hungry and ordered a medium pizza. After we ate that pizza, we ordered a small pizza, thinking our hunger would be subdued. It wasn't. I was running out of money, so I ordered each of us a mini pizza. We devoured those and were still hungry. We were both in our early twenties and skinny as rails. I have no idea how we ate that much pizza without getting sick.

Later that night, there was to be a dance at my dorm. CJ and I met our friends Jack and Jill (yes, those were their real names) at the dance. After an hour or so, we all decided to order some snacks and sodas. We found our table and sat down. A good band was playing that night, so the place was unusually packed. The tables all around us were full of guys and their dates.

I liked Cracker Jack back then, so that's what I ordered. I have a tendency to save until the end the things I enjoy eating the most. With Cracker Jack, it was the peanuts. I had a little pile of peanuts pushed off to the side, and I was planning to eat them after the popcorn was gone.

My wife is a beautiful redhead. She is the one every guy in the room would like to be sitting next to. I was that special guy lucky enough to be sitting next to that beauty. Suddenly, that beautiful redhead reached over and started picking up my peanuts.

To this day, I don't know why I did it, but I yelled out rather loudly so almost everyone could hear me.

"Don't grab my nuts!"

Almost immediately, I realized what I said and wished I hadn't. It was too late. The whole place got quiet. I wanted to get away, but there was no hiding. My table of friends was doing nothing to help me. They were laughing hysterically.

No one had to say anything. It was the perfect background. A bunch of college kids were sitting at a table in a noisy room enjoying their surroundings. Suddenly someone yelled what young people would easily misinterpret as a sexual innuendo. It's just one of those uncontrollable things that happen to all of us.

My wife enjoys relating this story whenever given the opportunity. I try not to make it too easy for her, though. To this day, I don't eat Cracker Jack.

The Army Physical

I spent seven years in the army. I am proud to have served my country. I have absolutely no regrets. During those years I was stationed at three different military installations. Although I am a Vietnam era veteran, I never served overseas. But that didn't mean my life was not going to forever change.

Every young man, when he enters the service, has a rude awakening. In the US Army, it is called Basic Combat Training. That awakening begins abruptly as you come off the bus and your feet hit the ground. Mine took place at Ft. Leonard, Missouri.

I and twenty other men took a bus from the St. Louis recruiting station and headed out for our first day as soldiers. *Soldiers* were what we called ourselves. We were sadly mistaken. We were recruits.

When we all arrived at Ft. Leonard Wood, it was cold, and there was about six inches of snow on the ground. All recruits were expected to line up in formation as they came off the bus. Never having been exposed to anything quite like that before, an obvious question needed to be asked. A young man with shoulder-length hair and a cigarette hanging out of his mouth, I think his name was Howard, was brave enough to ask it. "Dude! What's a formation?"

Although I would not have asked it that way, I was so glad I was not the one who asked that question.

Some old guy in a green uniform and a brown, wide brimmed state trooper hat ran over to that long haired boy, yanked the cigarette out of his mouth, and started screaming profanities at the poor guy.

The young man was petrified. So was I, for that matter.

It took a minute or two before the state trooper was able to place Howard where he was supposed to be. I was placed next to him. Fifteen minutes later, in actuality more like five minutes, we were amazingly in formation, four rows with five recruits in each row.

That state trooper's fun was just beginning. He really wasn't a state trooper. We were in the army. Don't know why I thought state trooper. Guess it was the hat. He was staff sergeant Ardemis Brown, and we were to address him as Drill Sergeant Brown.

That obnoxious Drill Sergeant Brown was not done screaming at Howard. All I could think about was, *I hope he doesn't start screaming in my face and knock me in the nose with the brim of that stupid hat like he's doing to the guy next to me.*

I certainly did not know what I would do if he screamed at me.

I had graduated from college a few weeks earlier. Based upon Drill Sergeant Ardemis Brown's vocabulary, I was pretty sure I had more intelligence than him. Judging by the reaction of that guy next to me, I decided to use some good ol' back home common sense. I was going to make myself invisible to that screaming sergeant.

Unbeknownst to all of the recruits, the drill sergeant had a plan. He was going to create chaos for every single recruit. No one was to escape.

But I did ... for about two weeks.

We were forming up for our march to Sunday service.

"Russey!" Drill Sergeant Brown was yelling at me.

"Sir, yes, sir?" I bellowed back. I had learned early on that he liked bellowing.

"Glad you decided to join us, Russey."

"Sir, yes, sir."

"Russey, don't ever decide to join us again if you can't come fully dressed."

"Sir, yes, sir, I won't, sir." I was totally confused.

I took a chance that Drill Sergeant Brown would show some compassion on this poor, confused recruit. I was wrong to think that way.

"Sir, what am I missing, sir?" I meekly asked. Asking anything meekly never worked. I knew better. I had seen others fall in disgrace whenever they answered anything in any way that resembled meekness.

The brim of his hat found my nose. I thought I could smell Listerine as he opened his mouth to begin his rant.

"Who gave you permission to question me? Just because you are a college graduate, you think you know better than me how to dress yourself. I bet your momma wouldn't let you leave the house like that. I've been in this man's army since Moses was a tadpole." That could not have been true, of course. I sure wasn't about to tell him that.

"Since you are a college man and can obviously read, you make sure you read the regs tonight about the exact placement of your name tag."

I glanced down and was horrified to see that the tag was pointing north and south instead of east and west. Apparently, I had not done a thorough enough check of my equipment before standing formation. I still think Drill Sergeant Ardemis Brown planned this encounter.

This military adventure and many others were not going to happen without first taking an entrance exam. That exam took place at the St. Louis, Missouri, recruiting station.

I very nearly missed out on the opportunity to serve in Uncle Sam's army. Here's what happened.

When I was in my last year of college, I received my formal invitation to take a military physical. On the date of my scheduled exam, I woke early, got in my car, and left for St. Louis, Missouri.

Soon after arrival in the recruiting station, I was ask to strip down to my skivvies, cough, pee in a cup, squat, and do a variety of other humiliating activities. My blood pressure was checked. Someone even checked my heart to ensure it was still ticking. A heart that was still ticking was obviously an important requirement for military service.

I had no problems passing everything asked of me. Passing the mental test would be no problem. I, after all, was a senior in college and no doubt knew more than any of those illiterate high school kids I was testing with.

One final exam was all I needed to pass the physical. I headed down another hallway to see Cpl. McMaster, a med tech who was to give me a vision test.

Unconcerned, I sat behind the vision tester. My dad, an optometrist, had given me a vision test the day before and declared me fit for service.

How could it be? I could not believe the words coming out of his mouth. "You failed; you've been found ineligible for the army. Go see the sarge next door, and he'll give you your next set of instructions."

This guy had to be an idiot. He was insulting my father. I could not let him get away with that.

"Wait a minute. You're wrong; my dad checked my eyes yesterday and said I have twenty-twenty vision. He's an optometrist. Let me see your doctor!"

I must have been the one hundred fifty-third recruit the med tech had seen that day. Cpl. McMaster had every right to ignore my request. Instead, for whatever reason, he sent me on to the optometrist.

The doctor was an older gentleman in a white smock who really didn't look or sound like he knew what he was doing. Perhaps I thought that because he was performing a screening, not a complete exam as my father had done the previous day. Or perhaps I was comparing him to the only eye doctor I knew, my father. It didn't matter anyway because he found me quite capable of serving our country.

I was thrilled. I successfully defended my father's honor and could not wait to tell him of my first adventure in the army. I was so proud.

Unfortunately, I cannot say the same for my father. He was not pleased with my determination to defend him. I had never before spent any large amount of time talking to my father about military service or about going to war. Dad had different feelings about the military than I did. He was not anti-Vietnam War, but he was not exactly promilitary either. He believed military personnel were second-class citizens. He also believed that anyone called into service should do the honorable thing. One should serve the time, get out at the earliest possible moment, and move on.

Dad saw my adventure as an opportunity to honorably avoid becoming a second-class citizen. Dad was willing, for his son's sake, to look incompetent. Cpl. McMaster had no influence on his life in any way.

Dad's response to my adventure was, "Bend over, son. Let me demonstrate what a size ten army boot really feels like. You had a chance to get out of this. Why didn't you take it?"

No more was ever said to me about what he perceived as a mistake. As far as he was concerned, I had to live with the consequences. I believe deep down, though, he was proud of me, both for defending him and for my service to our country.

I did pass the physical and moved on to the next chapter in my life, the military. That's another story.

time. You could not stroke him again if you valued your fingers.

Shannon also let it be known to me in no uncertain terms that my future wife, CJ, was his momma. I was not to get near her as long as he was around. If CJ and I would sit on the couch, Shannon would jump up and get between us. He would sit there, looking up at me with a smirk until I moved somewhere else. That little ten-pound dog had this strapping young man of eighteen scared to death. It didn't help that CJ and her family treated him like he was the king. I honestly thought that dog believed he was a king, and wherever he was, he considered it his kingdom.

CJ, Shannon, and I had a lengthy courtship. After about four years, I finally asked my wife to marry me. Not only did I have to get the approval of CJ's parents, but it was also very important I had won the approval of the king. This had to be done because I was taking CJ away from him. I knew we would be coming back for visits, and I needed to be sure the king would be okay with it. If I didn't have his approval, I might be doctoring my fingers and toes.

Feeling confident I had satisfied everyone, a date was set and plans were made.

The day of our wedding finally arrived. It went off without a hitch except for one thing. Throughout the ceremony, thoughts of that dog, King Shannon, kept creeping into my brain. I knew it was wrong to think about a dog on my wedding day, but I had no control over how that crazy dog would react when he found out what was about to happen.

Our first night together as husband and wife was to be spent in the home of my new in-laws. As you can imagine, spending the wedding night in the home of in-laws is an invitation for much consternation. CJ and I, the newly married couple of only a few hours, were looking forward to the start of our honeymoon the next morning. All we had to do was make it through the night.

Somehow, Shannon figured out I was not leaving that night. He hung around to ensure all was right in his world. I complicated it when he realized I was going to sleep in his bed. You see, my new wife failed to inform me of one small detail. Shannon was used to sleeping in bed with her, so he was going to do whatever he could to make sure I did not sleep in his bed. My night was about to become more uncomfortable than it already was.

I made it through the night in my wife's bed but not without some trials and tribulations. Remember, I was a newlywed and about to sleep in the same house as my in-laws and that scary dog. As you can imagine, I was anxious about this night for many reasons.

My wife's bedroom was also the family room. This room had no doors. Her bed was the foldout couch. No newlywed business was happening that night. I had already figured that out. Didn't matter to Shannon.

When I finally worked up the courage to get in bed with my new wife and kiss her good night in this very public forum, Shannon magically appeared. He jumped on to the bed, squirmed between our faces, put his butt next to my nose, and farted. Aargh! Whatever thoughts I had of romance that night were just blown away.

If I still needed any convincing of Shannon's ability to talk, this next adventure absolutely made a believer of me. Shannon was about to speak very clearly.

I was stationed for a few years at Fort Leonard Wood, Missouri. CJ and I lived off base in a trailer court. The base was about four hours from her home. CJ's parents and the king would come for frequent visits. We looked forward to those visits. Her dad would always take us out to eat. That was a good thing for newly married people on an army private's income.

By this time, Shannon had finally come to accept me as a member of his family. That, of course, made his visit with me a little less stressful. Even though he came to my kingdom to visit, he was still in charge. He told me that every time he came for a visit. I never challenged his authority over me.

A terrible thing happened to Shannon on one of his visits, and everyone in his world paid the consequences. He was ruthless with his reprimands.

The day started out as all other days of visits began. As usual, we left the trailer for the trek to the local KFC and Walmart. Trips to Walmart were a very big deal for us back then. This ritual would usually last four to five hours. Before leaving, we would make sure King Shannon's personal needs were taken care of. The king had no problems with this routine. He would gleefully greet us upon our return.

On this Sunday afternoon, the routine was unknowingly changed. We humans tried to ruin King Shannon's life. That's what he told us.

On that fateful day, we returned from town, opened the trailer door, and... no Shannon. We hesitated at the door for a moment. Perhaps the king was sleeping and didn't hear us yet. We certainly did not want to rudely wake our king. We quietly called out our king's name. No answer. We entered his domain and called out his name a little louder. Still no answer. A little louder now... no answer.

We all were getting somewhat concerned. Maybe he got out. He was an old dog. Maybe he was not able to come to us anymore.

The family quickly spread out over the trailer, calling his name. Richard, my father-in-law, remained on watch at the open door. Maybe Shannon had somehow managed to get out and was waiting for us to return.

CJ and her mother headed through the living room for the kitchen. I headed down the hallway to check the bedroom and bathroom. The doors were closed. We never closed them when we left. It was his kingdom, and he had access to it all.

Nothing was happening in the kitchen or living room. Nothing happened when I opened the bedroom door. I thought I heard a noise coming from the bathroom. I opened the door, and all I can remember is a little brown fuzzy ball flying past me, heading for the open door. It was King Shannon. In a blink of an eye, he was through the open door and in the road taking care of his business.

I guarantee it is not what you are thinking.

King Shannon was telling the entire trailer park

that his subjects tried to usurp his power. How dare us try to do such a terrible thing? Each and every one of us, his devoted subjects, told King Shannon the moment we saw him in the street how sorry we were. We pleaded with him for forgiveness. The more we pleaded, the madder he got.

My father-in-law was especially sorry. You see, he was the last one in the bathroom. He was unaware that King Shannon was visiting the throne room. Apparently, Richard allowed the door to close behind him and did not know Shannon would be captured inside.

Our pleading did not matter to the king. With smoke coming from his ears, he sat there in the street and cussed us out for the next fifteen solid minutes. Oh! The vulgarity that oozed from his lips. Every single car entering the park stopped. I am sure to this day that the people in those cars had never heard such language.

Then, just as suddenly as his tirade began, it was over. He told us we were never to speak of this to him again. And we never did.

Now, how can you read this and not admit that Shannon did not talk?

Post Card

Firstborn

Birthing babies is not a topic men generally talk much about. But birthing babies is certainly an adventure worth talking about. Any man who has ever taken fatherhood seriously cannot avoid the baby birthing adventures.

In late 1974, my wife and I found out we were going to be blessed with our first child. We were stationed at Fort Leonard Wood, Missouri, then.

As pregnancy goes, I don't remember it being any different than what most people say they experience in a normal pregnancy. The young lady who was actually physically experiencing this birth, my wife, may have something different to say about it being a normal pregnancy. Even though I may have given a different impression to others, as a first-time father, I didn't really know what to expect.

One night will, for me, forever stand out. It was the day of delivery.

On that blessed day I went to work as usual. For some reason, CJ told me that I ought to be ready to come home early from work. Her maternal clock must have been clanging. Anyway, late in my workday the expected call came from my wife. I grabbed my hat and excused myself. I believed I was prepared. I had, after all, successfully completed a Lamaze class with my wife.

CJ and I were in the labor room when my horrifying adventure began.

CJ was just beginning to have hard contractions as

we got settled into our room. I was new to this birthing baby thing, so I had no idea what to expect in a labor room. All I knew was that it was a place a very pregnant, expectant mother and her husband would go to just before the delivery of their baby.

For me, the labor room was scary. There was a bed, some medical equipment, and some wires. Someone in white, a nurse I think, hooked up something that looked like a piece of sonar equipment from a submarine to my wife's belly. As soon as it was turned on, I heard a pinging sound. That was a strange sound for an army man to hear. My pregnant wife didn't seem to be much concerned about the sonar equipment. I learned to trust her, so I put my concerns aside.

The expectant mother was relaxed. I was mentally going over the instructions given to us in our Lamaze classes. I was preparing for the time when I would have to count, wipe her brow, comfort her, etc. I could handle it. No sweat. My wife had all the work to do.

From somewhere, I didn't immediately know where, I heard what sounded like a woman's scream, followed by "You *moron!*"

CJ heard it too because she was as wide-eyed as I must have been. We were both quiet, trying to figure out what we just heard and how that related to our environment. I guess it was the fight-or-flight thing.

"You *idiot*. Don't you ever touch me again."

I swear I saw a slight smile on my wife's face.

My brain by now was about frazzled. A lady screaming at someone, my wife smiling, and the sonar equipment attached to her belly was pinging away. Way too much information for my brain to process.

Then CJ took my hand and started squeezing. What was I supposed to do? Oh yeah! That was the signal a contraction was beginning, and I had to keep track of the time. I could do that.

Another bloodcurdling scream.

About then I figured out where all this commotion was coming from. It was from across the hall. Another expectant couple was in that room.

My concentration was broken. I wasn't prepared for what my mind thought it was going to see.

"You frigging moron. You're the reason I hurt like this. Don't you ever get near me again, or I'll make sure you can't do this to me again."

At this point, I was extremely worried about what CJ was going to do. Remember the movie *The Exorcist*? I was trying to comfort her as best I could while at the same time I was waiting on my wife to do the Linda Blair thing. You know, where her head does a 360?

CJ was starting to laugh now. I was looking at her head.

Once again the yelling could be heard from across the hall.

I was scared out of my wits. What was going to happen here? I was sweating profusely; I didn't know what to do. I certainly couldn't ask my wife. She was smiling at me.

Her mouth began to form a word. I thought she was about to speak.

"That lady across the hall from us is an RN and has a six-week rotation in the OB ward. You'd think she'd have a better understanding of what's going on than the rest of us. She ought to know better than to be screaming like that. Her husband is a soldier stationed here. He has to take all that from someone who should know what to expect. Poor guy.

"You looked kind of worried. You didn't really pay any attention to that stuff, did you?"

"What? Me? No, of course not, honey. Why would I?"

Our son, Pierre Jacque Russey II, was delivered into the world a few short hours later.

Pete was a blessing in our lives. After nine short months, he succumbed to a childhood disease. We still miss him.

Fishing on the Rebedeoux

I'm not much of a fisherman. In fact, you could say I'm not a fisherman at all. But I do have a fishing story. This adventure involves my cousin Jake and me.

At the time of this adventure, Jake was an avid fisherman. Today, he still has the desire but no longer has the opportunities. When this story took place, he was so into fishing that he even made his own lures. In my opinion, anyone who would spend much of his free time making his own lures and then brag about them is extremely hooked on fishing. I could not understand the effort he put into making those lures.

When I asked my cousin why he made his lures instead of buying them, he simply said, "The fish can tell the difference." Huh. I guess his fish had discriminating taste buds. Who was I to dispute him? He was getting a great deal of enjoyment from his hobby.

My cousin served in the army before I joined and was responsible for bringing me in before he left it. Jake was stationed at Fort Leonard Wood, Missouri, his entire tour of duty. He left the army two months before I became active duty. I eventually took over his job.

Ft. Leonard Wood was a wonderful place to live. There was plenty of opportunity to fish, so Jake managed to find a way to stay in the area a while after his military service was over. He became a civilian teacher on the base.

When I was finally stationed there as my permanent assignment, I moved off base to the same trailer court where my cousin and his wife were living. The trailer court only had about fifteen trailers in it. I liked it because it was away from the base and didn't have many people living there. I did not then nor do I now enjoy being around a lot of people. Living on base meant dealing with congestion. I was also happy to be in the same neighborhood with my cousin.

Jake is five years older and a full foot taller. He was twenty-eight when I became his neighbor and looked like the same handsome six-foot-six high school jock he was ten years earlier.

Doing things together as a youth was difficult. Jake was already in college by the time I started high school. Even though we lived in the same town growing up, a freshman in high school had very little in common with a college freshman.

By the time I moved into my cousin's neighborhood, we were both adults, and the age spread didn't seem to matter as much. Having a few adventures together would be fun.

One activity we could easily do together was fishing. I didn't really like to, but I enjoyed my cousin's company. Jake would fish, and I would pretend I was interested.

One summer, we planned a one-day float trip down the Rebedeoux River. It was located a few miles from us. This was going to be some serious fishing.

Jake decided I needed practice before we floated the river. He took us to a local farmer's pond two or three days earlier to try to teach me the proper technique of fishing from a raft. We fished from the bank of the pond. I am not sure how that provided me with raft fishing experience. Personally, I think it was just an excuse for him to fish.

Teaching me how to fish at that pond had to be an aggravation for Jake. I would cast, and my line would get tangled in a nearby tree. It would happen more than once or twice. Jake did not offer to help me untangle the line. I guess he thought that since I put it in the tree it was my responsibility to get it back.

After a couple more hours of casting, my cousin and I thought I had the hang of it, but he wanted to fish a few more minutes before we packed up to go back home. We were fishing pretty close to each other most of the night. He must have figured that was the safest place to be.

Jake told me I was ready for a casting challenge. He walked about twenty feet away and pointed down to his feet. A big bullfrog was croaking at his feet near the water's edge. The fact that my cousin was in its space didn't seem to concern the bullfrog. I thought that was strange. But who am I to question a bullfrog.

Jake told me to cast toward the frog and get as close to it as I could. He must have been pretty confident of this fishing newbie, and that made me feel confident also.

With a flick of my wrist, I cast in the direction of the frog. I watched as the line flew out of my fishing rod. In less time than it took to wink, I knew there was going to be a problem. There was nothing I could do about it now.

All I could do was watch the hook to see where it was going. Jake was going to be very disappointed with me.

The result of my casting challenge was going to land nowhere near the frog.

Suddenly that big, strapping young man was yelping like a coyote.

Oh! Great! I hooked his ear.

I have to admit, watching him dance was hilarious. But I didn't dare laugh. Jake was a whole lot bigger and stronger than me. My main concern was staying out of his reach. I wasn't convinced he wouldn't try to use me as fish bait.

That pretty much put an end to the night's fishing. Even after demonstrating my lack of expertise, the float trip was still on. He didn't appear to be worried one little bit. Jake was a brave man.

The day finally came for the float trip. We packed Jake's car with all the equipment he thought we would need. Jake knew what he was doing. He and friends had made the exact same float before.

There must have been about ten different rods and reels, five or six fishing lines of various weights (one of them looked like it was for a whale), some kind of gadget that measured depth, a rubber raft, and one paddle. Of course we loaded his favorite tackle box and some soft drinks.

As we were packing, a question came to mind. I was kind of curious as to how we were going to get his car since it was to be left at the entry point of the float and we were going to be twenty miles away from it at the end of the float. I thought it was a good question, since I really had no desire to walk that far on a hot summer day.

Jake had it planned but didn't tell me before the trip because he assumed I already knew. To him, it was logical. That would not be the first time that day he would make a wrong assumption.

I was told to leave my car at the place where we would exit the river. We would then pack the stuff into my car and drive back to his. Sounded like a perfectly logical plan to me.

After loading up, we told our wives what time to expect us to return, said good-bye, got into our respective vehicles, and headed out. My car was left at the preplanned location. I got into his car, and we drove to a location twenty miles away. When we arrived at the spot where we were to put in, I told my cousin the river looked low to me. In fact, I was concerned that we were going to have to portage a time or two. Jake assured me the river never got that low.

Jake pulled his car off the road so we could unload. It really wasn't a parking space. It was more of a flat grassless area. It looked like others had used this spot to do the same thing we were about to do. The raft and gear were unloaded, and away we went.

We were going to spend the next few hours floating downstream and catching lots of fish. The quality time together was something we both looked forward to.

The Rebedeoux was quiet. The day was hot, but we didn't notice. The river was well shaded, and after a few minutes of rafting in the water, we acclimated to the temperature. I honestly can't remember how many fish, if any, were caught. We were enjoying the quiet of our surroundings.

We had floated a little over halfway to our destination when my cousin broke the silence to ask *the* question of the trip. Why he waited until that particular moment, neither of us really knew.

"Pete, do you have your car keys?"

"What a stupid question." I felt my right front pocket where I usually kept them, just to be sure. "Of course I…" I started exploring other pockets. "Uh-oh. I can't find them. They're not in my pocket where I usually put them."

I patted myself down some more before I finally realized what I did with them.

"Jake, my wise and wonderful, favorite cousin, we have a problem, and you're not going to be happy with me. I think I locked them in your car."

Jake had made another wrong assumption. He didn't think I would be stupid enough to do what I did. That's the problem with not being close. My wife would have assumed me to be that stupid and would not have allowed me to get in the raft without first checking my pants.

This float trip took place around 1974, before the existence of cell phones. We were virtually helpless. There was no way we could contact anyone. At least we had a couple more hours to figure something out.

I remember Jake as a rather mild mannered individual. But at that moment I was pretty sure I could see smoke coming from his ears. Kind of like you see in the cartoons. Fortunately for me, he took a few seconds to think about his response.

"Pete," he said, "I have the solution to your problem. When we get back to your car, I will give you my keys, and you can walk the twenty miles back to my car to get your keys and then drive back here to pick me up. I'll just fish some more until you get back."

Jake reached up to his ear, the one with the Band-Aid. It had to be a reminder of his stupidity for teaching his ignorant cousin how to fish.

I could have complained, but what good would it have done? I just hoped that he wasn't serious about making me walk that twenty miles. I had a couple of hours to worry about how my wonderful, awesome, kind cousin was going to make me pay for this.

The rest of the trip was spent in silence. I could hear our raft pushing the water away as we traveled down the Rebedeoux. What worried me the most was that smile on Jake's face.

When we finally arrived at our destination, we pulled the raft out of the river together. My kind and wonderful cousin gave me one more chance to hopefully reverse our misfortune. He suggested that maybe my car was unlocked and my keys were still there. I was sure hoping he was right. I wasn't going to be such an idiot then. But I was. Now there was no doubt my keys were twenty miles away from us.

I had no idea how we were going to get home, but my cousin did. He used those few hours of silence to formulate his plan. Now he was going to implement it.

Jake told me that since my keys were the problem, I was to hit the road. I had just been asked to do something I had never done in my life. I had to flag a car down and ask whoever was driving it to take me back to the trailer court. I believe it's called hitchhiking. Once back at the trailer court, I was to roust out his wife, explain my stupidity to her, and have her pick him up. Oh yeah! I was to ride with her and bring my car keys. He was going to stay with my car next to the river and fish.

So I started walking. My car was parked a few hundred feet down a dirt road from the interstate. Reaching the interstate meant it was about ten miles back to the trailer court. At least the walking distance had been cut in half.

I was aggravated and hot. I was already sweating. Cars were whizzing by me. Once in a while I would get a warm breeze when a vehicle would pass by a little too close for comfort. I sure hoped someone would stop and pick me up. I hoped I wouldn't get mugged by whoever picked me up. How stupid could I be? What kind of abuse was I going to take from the girls? It sure was hot. I hoped I didn't have to walk much farther.

I was deep in self-pity when I realized a car was pulling up behind me. The window rolled down, and out popped my cousin's head. Not what I expected. How did he do that?

Apparently, Jake has a bit more luck than I do. I was not gone more than fifteen minutes, and some guy pulled up next to my locked car, fishing gear in hand. The guy happened to be a friend of Jake's. My cousin explained his problem. The guy offered to take Jake back to town. Fortunately for me, Jake was not able to implement his plan. That guy convinced my cousin to pick me up.

Needless to say, by the time we arrived back at the trailer court two hours late, we had a lot of explaining to do.

It would be a long time before my cousin let me live it down.

Neighborly Love

In my four decades as an adult, I have moved many times from 1968 to 2000. I have had thirty-five mailing addresses. That, of course, means I have had many neighbors.

In 1977, the army saw fit to move me to Fort Bliss, Texas. It was there that I had a most unusual experience with neighborly love.

Fort Bliss is located in El Paso, Texas. My wife and I grew up in small towns and are not particularly promoters of the big city life. To us, El Paso was going to be a challenge. Until we moved there, the largest city we lived in was about 20,000 people. El Paso had several hundred thousand more. Consequently, we didn't like that city.

I remember the first time we entered El Paso. It was a dark spring night. We were driving south down Interstate 10 from New Mexico. As we approached the city, I looked down the hill and saw a couple of lights. I thought maybe they were farmhouses. I knew Juarez, Mexico, was close to El Paso. Maybe we were approaching Juarez.

Looking up and to the other side of the interstate, I saw the University of Texas El Paso. Coming out of the darkness of the night, I thought, *Wow, that is one beautiful school*. We had been driving a very long time, and seeing that well-lit architectural beauty in the still of the night was awe-inspiring.

Sometime later, my wife and I had a chance to travel that same route in daylight hours. What a difference the sunlight makes. This time when I looked to the Mexico side, we saw what looked like thousands and thousands of cardboard shanties. It was not a suburb I saw that first night. It was Juarez, Mexico.

I now had a different impression of the area. Above me was the beautiful campus of the University of Texas El Paso. Below me was the residence of several thousand people who did not exist to me in the dark of night. I was struck with the irony. The king of the hill was looking down on his subjects. Affluence above me and abject poverty below me.

Neither my wife nor I liked living in El Paso. It was hot all the time. There was always lots of traffic. For a big city, it didn't seem to offer much in the way of entertainment. The exception was eating establishments. There was a large variety of fast food and sit down restaurants. To this day, I believe one could eat three meals a day every day of the year and still not have eaten at every restaurant. We managed to eat at many of them.

CJ and I lived on base for the first and only time in my military career. I wonder if our experience was typical of life on a military base, or was our experience here just unusual?

El Paso's climate is hot and dry. We frequently commented on the lack of vegetation. In fact, we would tell our friends and family back east that the only things sticking out of the ground were rocks and plastic trees.

Our neighborhood could pretty much be described the same way, with one exception. We had lots of green-colored cockleburs in our backyard, rendering it virtually useless for any sort of activity.

All the houses in the neighborhood were shaped about the same. They were single-story ranch-style homes. Ours had two bedrooms and one bath. What I remember most about it was the big room off the kitchen. It was a combination living room and dining room.

We lived in that house eighteen months.

One time, we asked if we were allowed to paint the inside walls. To our amazement we were told we could, but we only had a choice of five colors. They were off-white, off-white, off-white, off-white, and off-white. Guess what color we picked.

Two of our neighbors were just plain weird. We lived on a corner lot and had neighbors on two sides of us. The neighbors' names were Smith and Wesson. They both had infantry specialties and worked with different types of weapons. The folks in the neighborhood thought the names Smith and Wesson were rather ironic. As you know, Smith and Wesson are weapons manufacturers. Here were two guys with those names living on a military base next to each other. All kinds of jokes were made about that.

The Smiths lived behind us, and the Wessons lived beside us. They lived in those homes before we moved into the neighborhood. The Wessons had five-year-old twin boys. The Smiths were childless. Both women were stay-at-home wives and were probably twenty-seven years old. My wife told me she guessed that to be their ages. Guys can't do that without severe consequences. So I believed her.

My wife commented one night that she thought Mrs. Wesson lifted weights. Although she looked slight in stature, her arms appeared as if she lifted weights. I told CJ it must be from hauling around her heavyweight twins. She always seemed to have one in each arm. And those boys were five.

The relationship between these two families was very volatile. Living between Smith and Wesson made our lives quite interesting. We did not need television. What we saw every night was better than any television theater.

Everyone in the neighborhood was a noncommissioned officer. Smith and Wesson worked at different locations on the base. As far as I knew, the only time they saw each other was after-duty hours.

For some reason, they did not like each other. Every night they displayed dislike of each other to the entire neighborhood. My goal while I lived between them was to find out why there was so much animosity. I left the army never knowing why.

Supper was usually peaceful. I guess time for them was needed to unwind from work and to prepare for the altercations that were about to begin.

Like clockwork, every day at 7:00 p.m. the entertainment would commence. Sgt. Smith would come out on his patio and begin glaring at SSgt. Wesson's house. About fifteen minutes later, SSgt. Wesson would dart out of his front door to the edge of his yard and start bad mouthing Sgt. Smith. Every night, Smith would deny any wrongdoings.

One night I could have sworn I heard Sgt. Wesson

complain to Sgt. Smith that Smith's wife had no business commenting about the size of his wife's arms.

Sometimes people just say stupid nonsensical things about each other.

Smith's response to Wesson went something like this. "Oh yeah! My wife can beat up your wife even though she has skinny arms." I couldn't believe I heard that. These guys were grown men, not kids.

I can't swear that's exactly what CJ and I heard, but it sure sounded something like that. It was that kind of stupid kid stuff every time they fought.

The banter would continue back and forth for approximately two hours. CJ and I lived between them so long that we would take turns reciting their lines before either of them would say them. Some nights, maybe if the atmosphere was just right, their voices would resonate throughout the entire neighborhood.

Occasionally, someone tired of their nightly routine and called the MPs. The MPs would arrive a few minutes later, break up the show for the night, and then leave. No citations were ever issued, as far as I know. It was almost as if the MPs actually enjoyed the visit to our neighborhood. Perhaps they looked upon this visit as a break from a mundane routine.

One day when I came home from work, my wife told me she got to watch a special episode of the Smith and Wesson show. This one featured only the wives and started shortly after I left for work.

CJ said the wives were yelling and screaming at each other out their back doors. It had something to do with a borrowed stereo. Apparently, the Smiths loaned their stereo to the Wessons. Now the Smiths needed the stereo back, and the Wessons were not willing to return it at that time.

CJ said the screaming continued until Mrs. Wesson finally threw the stereo out her back door and told Mrs. Smith to come and get it. Mrs. Smith called the MPs. They came with red lights flashing. Mrs. Smith told the MPs she was being threatened by Mrs. Wesson and was afraid for her life.

The MPs loaded both of them into separate cars and took them away. CJ says every time she sees the TV show *America's Most Wanted* and watches the bad guys get loaded into the squad cars, she is reminded of those two housewives from Ft. Bliss.

Mrs. Smith was brought back to her house a couple hours later. Mrs. Wesson had to be released to her husband's custody later that night.

That was a quiet night in the neighborhood. Apparently, SSgt. Wesson was filling out paperwork so he could bring his wife back home.

The Smith and Wesson show was off the air for only about a week before it returned to its regularly scheduled time.

One night, the show stopped. For two or three weeks, no one saw Smith or Wesson. No one had a clue. Our favorite TV show had been yanked from the airwaves.

What were we supposed to do now?

How were we going to fill that void we learned to depend upon so much?

Then, one night, a new Smith and Wesson Show

began playing. It had the same characters, but the script was entirely different. In this show, the main characters enjoyed one another's company. They were laughing together, and it appeared they were anxious to see each other.

Something had happened to change the script.

Mrs. Smith, SSgt. Wesson's sister, just had a baby boy. Actually, Sgt. and Mrs. Smith had been trying for years to have a child. The arrival of the child softened the hearts of the two warring parties. Smith and Wesson were now inseparable.

The military police never visited the neighborhood again, and I never did find out what all their fuss was about.

The End of an Era

I was transferred to Ft. Bliss, Texas, from Ft. Leonard Wood, Missouri, because I had changed my MOS, military occupational specialty. Instead of being a file clerk as I was before, I decided I would take one more stab at following in my father's optometric footsteps.

The military gave me the opportunity. All I had to do was first go through Basic Combat Medic training at Ft. Sam Houston in San Antonio, Texas. Other than the actual training itself, the six months CJ and I spent there were fantastic.

San Antonio is a nice town, except for the weather. When we lived there, San Antonio had five military installations, so most people were familiar with military personnel. No matter where you went, there was someone nearby from the military. Finding common things to talk about was easy.

It has been nearly thirty years since I have been back, so I imagine the city has changed somewhat. I'm sure many modern upgrades have been made to the River Walk. If you have not seen it, you must. CJ and I enjoyed floating up and down the canal on the Venice-style boats. That was always romantic. I even splurged once and bought us a dinner cruise. CJ was surprised. I, unfortunately, don't do enough of that sort of thing.

As beautiful as San Antonio was, it could at times be miserably hot. I know that firsthand because I had to several times run in that miserable heat with a full military pack.

Because I was training to be a combat medic, I needed to be in good physical shape, or at least that's what Staff Sergeant Brown, my training sergeant, kept telling me.

One hot August day, my training company ran, as usual, to the PT field two miles away in full gear. The gear consisted of a complete uniform, which we had to wear while running, combat boots, a white T-shirt for calisthenics, and our backpacks. I can't remember what was in the packs. All I remember is that they were heavy. My guess is the army commissioned the manufacturer of the backpacks to make them out of a secret material that got heavier with each item placed in it.

We left relatively early in the morning, so the heat was not an issue. Returning to our barracks four hours later was unpleasant. The summer sun was directly overhead and bearing down on us like it was angry at us. San Antonio's summers are hot and humid. I would venture to say that this day was over ninety degrees with 90 percent humidity or more. Running in full gear is not fun at all. Don't care who you are.

There was one soldier, though, who did seem to enjoy this particular run. It was our first day on the job, training officer, Second Lt. Travis. He was a wiry little guy and full of himself. He ran us the entire two miles in full gear, back into the parade ground in front of our barracks, and dead stopped us. He then called us to attention and had us remain at attention in formation.

The guys started dropping like flies. The lieutenant

chewed on each one even as they were falling to the pavement.

After about five minutes I saw something I never saw again the rest of my time in the army. Our training sergeant coolly walked over the Lt. Travis and almost put the big brim of his hat on the lieutenant's nose. I couldn't hear everything said, but I thought I heard things like, "Sir, you are an idiot, sir. You're crazy to run the unit in here and dead stop them and bring them to attention, sir." I was too busy trying not to pass out to be certain of what I heard.

Second Lt. Travis was outraged. "I'm an officer. You cannot talk to me like that. Cpt. Miller will hear about this."

Sgt. Brown simply said, "Sir, we shall see."

I remembered thinking, *Poor guy, I bet his career is over.* I was sure we would never see Brown again. I liked him too.

The next day, it was training as usual. But this time, Second Lt. Travis did not accompany us on our run. Our training officer was transferred out of the unit the next day. Apparently, Brown was right to chew out that wet-nosed lieutenant.

About three weeks later, I graduated from Basic Combat Medic Training and was shipped off to Ft. Bliss, located in El Paso, Texas. It was there that I was to complete training as an optometric assistant.

The final stage of my military career was about to unfold in El Paso, Texas.

Ft. Bliss was the opposite of my Ft. Sam Houston experience. Both CJ and I enjoyed the city where Ft.

Sam Houston was, but I didn't care much for the military experience.

On the other hand, neither CJ nor I liked El Paso much, but I enjoyed my military time there. Ft. Bliss had a training hospital, and I was assigned to it. It was there that I met Dr. Goodnight.

Dr. Goodnight was a resident intern who was trying to decide which medical field he was going to practice in. I was immediately impressed with him. He was probably in his late twenties or early thirties. I thought he kind of looked like Clint Eastwood.

Whenever I talked to him though, Dr. Goodnight spoke to me with an air of superiority. But that I could overlook. He was an officer, and I was an enlisted man.

When I met him, he was exploring ophthalmology as a career field. I only worked with him one day, and I will never forget him. Here is the story.

Mrs. Jackson, an elderly lady recently widowed, was scheduled to have a sty removed from her right eyelid that day. I remember Mrs. Jackson as being a petite lady who was soft spoken but full of energy. Dr. Goodnight was to be her surgeon. Removing a sty was minor outpatient surgery. This would be the first time he did any kind of eye surgery. My job was to prepare Mrs. Jackson for the operation.

I talked with Mrs. Jackson several times before. She was a pleasant and uncomplaining lady. I always enjoyed our conversations as I did on this day.

I cleansed Mrs. Jackson's right eyelid with sterile soap and water as I was instructed to do. I laid out the surgical equipment on a sterile tray for Dr. Goodnight. I then told the good doctor that his patient was prepped and ready for surgery.

Dr. Goodnight entered and began. I was to be available to him to fetch and carry. I was amazed at his surgical skills and still am.

The good doctor picked up the syringe to deaden Mrs. Jackson's eyelid and prepared to insert the needle into the patient's affected area. Just before inserting, he stopped in midair. He looked down at his hand and noticed he had failed to put on his gloves.

Nothing was said, but I can imagine what he was thinking. *Geez, I forgot the gloves. Need to put them on or I'll contaminate the area.*

I watched him start to place the syringe back on the tray to get his gloves, but just before the syringe touched the tray, he stopped again. His hand started back to the patient, syringe in hand. It was almost as if he was thinking.

It'll be okay. I didn't touch the needle. Once again, he stopped just before he reached Mrs. Jackson's eye.

He must have thought, *My hands are not sterile without the gloves. I better put them on.* He laid the syringe down, put on his gloves, picked up the syringe, and headed once again for poor Mrs. Jackson's eyelid. Just before contact, he stopped again.

I could hardly stand it. I wanted to laugh. What I was seeing was like something out of a comedy. But it wasn't. It was a real-life happening. Poor Mrs. Jackson! I really wanted to say something, but there was nothing I could do. He was an officer and I was enlisted.

Finally, he put the syringe back on the tray and asked me to get him a sterile syringe. He said it like it was my fault he was looking like an idiot.

I left the room to get him a new syringe.

When I returned, the chief surgeon entered to evaluate Dr. Goodnight's performance. Thankfully, the chief surgeon excused me from the rest of the surgery. Quite frankly, I did not know how much more I was going to be able to take.

I was instructed to stay in the adjoining room just in case I would be needed. A couple of minutes later, I heard Mrs. Jackson. "Ouch! It hurts, it hurts!"

Dr. Goodnight replied, "It can't hurt. It's been anesthetized."

"It hurts! It hurts!"

The chief surgeon abruptly appeared in the room where I was awaiting further instruction, and then he ordered me to go home.

I later found out that Dr. Goodnight was trying to perform surgery on Mrs. Jackson's left eyelid before he was stopped and relieved of his assignment.

I never saw the good doctor again. That's what really happened. You can't make that kind of stuff up. Sometimes I wonder where he is and what he is doing.

Although my wife and I were not big fans of El Paso, we did enjoy and appreciated much of what happened to us and around us while we lived there. We developed a strong friendship with another military couple, Sp5 Ben Smithton and his wife, Jackie. They were about our age and were from a very small town in eastern Texas.

Ben worked at the clinic while I worked at the hospital.

Our friendship was immediate. We did many activities together.

One such activity we planned to do together was snow skiing near Cloudcroft, New Mexico. Neither of us had ever done it and were eager to try. Ben made the arrangements and I drove.

Ben was one of those guys who just sort of stood out above the crowd. He was six-foot-seven and looked like a linebacker for the Chicago Bears. Ben was a funny guy, and he liked to be noticed. Showing up at a ski slope wearing a red and white paisley ski jacket certainly brought him many stares. To this day I have no idea where that jacket came from, and he never did share that information.

It became obvious right away that Ben was not made for skiing. We were going to put on our skis at the beginners' area before we attempted the slope. Ben reached down for his skis. I gave him a gentle, friendly shove. I guess I shoved too hard. He lost his balance. His skis were slightly behind him. Don't know why he did it, but as he was falling, he tried to reach for his skis. That action brought his head down toward his feet.

As he hit the snow, he curled up into a ball and started rolling head over heels, the snow gathering around him. Down the hill he went, picking up more snow and increasing his speed. Everyone on the slope did a double take. It isn't often that one sees a red and white paisley giant snowball rolling down a hill.

Although Ben liked to be the center of attention, he was so embarrassed he convinced me to leave. I don't think he ever tried to ski again.

A few months later CJ and I found out that she was pregnant.

The Christmas season of 1978, my second birthing baby adventure occurred. Richard Theron Russey was born. He was named after CJ's dad and my dad.

CJ was due to deliver in mid-December, so we decided not to go home for Christmas that year. There might have been a chance our son would be born on the plane when he decided to come out and play. If that happened, what would we put on his birth certificate as his place of birth?

CJ's parents decided to come out to El Paso to spend Christmas with us. They bought their tickets, boarded the plane, and safely arrived in sunny El Paso, Texas, on Christmas Eve.

On the day we were to pick them up, CJ was already a little over one and a half weeks past the due date. To the untrained eye (and, of course, mine was trained), she looked like she could deliver at any instant. I don't know how her belly could have stretched any farther. The expectant mother was not having any problems and was excited to see her parents.

They landed midmorning. We met them in the lobby of the airport. As they approached us, her dad's eyes were the only things we could see. If they were any larger, they would have plopped out.

Richard didn't even say hello. He looked at my wife's belly, grabbed her by the elbow, and said, "We've got to go to the hospital now! Why are you here?"

CJ calmly assured her dad that she wasn't having any discomfort. She was not going to deliver for a while.

I didn't show any stress, and CJ's mom didn't either, so Richard felt better. We gathered up their bags, loaded them in the car, and headed for the nearest Kentucky Fried Chicken for lunch. KFC was his favorite place to eat. He was going to pay, so what were we going to say?

After lunch, we drove them around some of the city. We drove down Dyer Street. It was a four-lane road with a thirty-five mile per hour speed limit. Everyone drove it at least fifty-five miles per hour. Richard told us he wanted to see the sites, so we had to slow down. Slowing down, for him, meant driving around ten to fifteen miles per hour. I tried it for about a minute. Horns honked, and we received a few one-finger salutes. I thought CJ was going to have the baby right on Dyer Street if I didn't relieve her stress. I got back up to everybody else's speed and vowed never to drive on that street that slowly again.

The next day was Christmas. The temperature was a balmy sixty degrees, so we ate our turkey outside on the patio. We still talk about the time we ate Christmas dinner on the patio in our shirtsleeves. That was the first and only time.

Unfortunately, I was unable to take off the entire time my in-laws were visiting. On the morning of the twenty-eighth of December, I was working on base when my father-in-law called to tell me CJ was headed to the hospital. CJ was going to have his grandson later that day. I asked if I could go home. My very "sympathetic" boss would not let me go. He wanted me to wait a couple of hours until the office was closed. I relayed that info to my father-in-law. A half hour later, Richard showed up at my office and was talking to my boss. Thirty minutes later, I was in the hospital waiting on Richard Theron to be born.

Fortunately, we had no problem with his birth. We brought him home two days later. Now, thirty years later, we are waiting once again for our son to come home. He is currently working in Europe. Maybe someday he and his family will come home to the good ol' US of A.

CJ and I lived in Fort Bliss for about three years. My seven years in the military ended there. We packed up our goods and headed back to southern Illinois where the next series of adventures were to begin as a civilian.

Civilian Again

The transition from soldier to civilian did not take long. I left the army in January 1980. The military provided me a comfortable living and time to raise a family. It taught me structure and discipline, two things I was severely lacking in my youth. Three months after leaving the army life, I had the opportunity to become a district executive for the Boy Scouts of America in familiar territory, southern Illinois.

Finding the job required me to use a great deal of that structure and discipline the army taught me. Up until this time, looking for employment was something I really never experienced. After high school, I immediately went to college. While in college I got called to go into the army. I didn't have any need to look.

I was able to enjoy freedom from the army for about one week. Then I realized it was time to buy the groceries. Many people provided me with a barrage of advice on how to seek employment. They told me I needed a résumé listing all my experiences and lots of patience. What the heck was a résumé, anyway? What kind of experience could I offer an employer?

Someone finally suggested I try to seek assistance from an employment agency. I looked in the phone book, closed my eyes, and let my finger select the one I would visit. I didn't realize it nor would I have ever admitted it back then, but I know now, I was led there by the hand of God.

My career counselor, Evelyn Shoulter I believe was her name, was a middle-aged woman. I think she owned the agency, or at least she presented herself as if she did. Carbondale, Illinois, where this employment agency was located, is a university town. I remember thinking that my counselor looked like she could have been a professor there at one time.

During the course of the initial interview, Evelyn said she had noticed I was in the Boy Scouts in my youth. She noticed I was an Eagle Scout. (Most people don't know what an Eagle Scout is but know it is very unusual to be talking to one.) I was caught off guard by her next question.

"Pete, have you ever considered working for the Boy Scouts?"

Huh! I thought. *Where'd that come from?*

I think my mouth must have dropped open. I couldn't answer her. How could I? Who ever heard of working for the Boy Scouts? You don't get paid to work for them; you enjoy being part of them. It's kind of like being on a high school baseball team. No one pays you to be on the team; you have fun being part of it. Anyway, those were my thoughts about that question.

"Pete, what do you think about working for the Boy Scouts?"

"Working for the Boy Scouts? You mean they pay people to do that?"

Evelyn explained to me that the local council was looking for a district executive. That person was responsible for bringing the scouting program to the youth in a specified geographical area. He (there was no she back then) would recruit boys for the program and raise money for it. The position, she told me, required a person with some knowledge of the scouting program, a college degree, and the ability to work well with others.

Evelyn suggested that because I had personal knowledge of it from the youth standpoint I might have an advantage in getting that position. She wasn't sure how long the job would be available, but I should definitely think about it.

For some reason, I really was not interested in working for the Boy Scouts of America. I had visions of me walking around in uniform with a bunch of kids. I would be wearing a neckerchief around my neck, shorts, and knee-high green socks with green tassels. I would know. That's what I ran around in when I was a scout. That was not what I had envisioned for my future. I just got out of a uniform.

I left her that day feeling pretty unhappy, but she made me promise I would talk it over with my wife and come back and see her in a couple of days.

This is where I had to begin applying the discipline and structure I learned in the army. The army taught me to do what I was told when I was told to do it. I set up an appointment with Evelyn and scheduled a return visit.

When I talked to CJ about my adventure at the employment agency, she was as confused as I was about what it meant to work for the Boy Scouts. We decided I needed a job and this was at least a lead.

The next day I called Evelyn and told her I would go on the interview.

Jerry Leighton was the guy I was to talk to about the district executive job.

Even though I had served in the military and had been on the abusive end of a sergeant's rant, Jerry still intimidated me. His feet were on his desk when I walked in. The chair must have been a good ten feet from the desk. Well, it seemed that way. Jerry left his feet up on that desk during the entire interview. Perhaps that's why he seemed so intimidating. Being a loud talker certainly added to that image. I presented him with my résumé Evelyn had helped me prepare.

Evelyn must have talked to him about me because I didn't think the interview process was particularly tough. Jerry made mention of my scouting and military background. He thought those would be excellent skills for a professional scouter.

There really wasn't much to the interview. I think he had already made his mind up about me before I even entered his office. Or maybe it was made up for him. He told me to go home and think about it and to call him back in a few days if I was interested. That was not the way job seeking was supposed to go. I had been told it was going to be a long, laborious adventure.

I told you I was led.

I was a Boy Scout in my youth, so I knew a little about the program. I enjoyed the boyhood time I spent in scouting. Now I had a chance to get paid to do something I loved doing when I was a kid. With my wife's consent, I decided to take the job.

A great deal of my time would be spent training youth and adults, so the Boy Scouts gave me the opportunity to finally use the teaching skills I learned in college. The discipline skills I learned while in the army were extremely beneficial when organizing Boy Scout activities, raising money, and recruiting membership in each district I served.

My first official day of employment for the BSA began on April Fool's Day. I will never forget the new job orientation I received from my new boss, Jerry Leighton.

He called me into his office and told me to sit down. I remembered that during the interview he was intimidating and to the point. At least this time his feet were on the floor. He did not indicate to me, then, he was the boss man. I didn't think to ask that question, and he did not volunteer that information either.

Mr. Leighton said to me, "Pete, you have five counties to manage. There are ten Explorer Posts, twenty-one Boy Scout troops, and twenty Cub Scout Packs. You have to raise twenty thousand dollars by year's end. This summer, you will be in charge of the summer camp program. In about six months you'll go to training at National Headquarters in Arlington, Texas. Col. Riley, your district chairman, can help you get started. There's the door. Now get to it." That was the end of my orientation. Evidently, I would have to learn to be an effective Scout executive on my own.

That night my head was spinning. *How many units did he say I had? How much money? He said something about a district chairman. What's a district chairman? He said it would be six to nine months before I would go to Texas to get my formal training. How am I supposed to get this stuff done without training? What in the world have I gotten myself into?*

The next day I found out how to get a hold of Col. Riley, and he made arrangements to meet me later that day. Col. Riley was retired Air Force. Like Jerry, he had a rather abrasive personality.

After I got to know him, we got along quite well.

The Colonel, as he was affectionately called, introduced me to a great number of the volunteers in my five-county area. In the beginning, he helped me organize units and meet the big money people.

Col. Riley was not always all business. He had a fun streak in him.

One day our council was asked to do a formal flag retreat at a regional adult leader training conference. The formal flag retreat was Col. Riley's responsibility. The Colonel appointed me along with himself and another volunteer to show up at retreat for the flag ceremony. The conference leaders called it a formal flag retreat, so we showed up in tuxedos and formally and respectfully lowered the flag. Everyone got a big kick out of it.

During the eight years as a professional scout, I managed three districts in two different states. The Russey family also added a daughter, Brianna, to the clan. Each time I took charge of a new district, I required my family to relocate to a new community. My son seemed to always enjoy meeting new people.

My wife and daughter didn't seem to get the same gratification out of the new environments as my son did.

The program aspect of the Boy Scouts of America provided me with a great deal of enjoyment. Showing young men how to become good citizens was not only rewarding for me but also, I believed, would make my father proud.

I am a slow learner and pretty much a perfectionist. I believe being a perfectionist is a trait I inherited from my father. So for most of my career in the Boy Scouts, I worked way too hard. Without exaggeration, I worked one hundred to 120 hours a week trying to reach the objectives my bosses laid out for me. I did not see much of my family anymore because I was out in the field. Because of that fact, it was my father-in-law who taught both my children to ride bicycles. I regret that.

My father had instilled in me, from an early age, the importance of loyalty to one's job. Working long hours was the only way I knew to prove loyalty to the most important thing in my life at that time, my job. My family would suffer for it.

Tight Pants

I became the Western District Executive for the Egyptian Council Boy Scouts of America. Impressive title, huh? After all these years, I still remember what my brother asked me after I told him of my title. He asked, "Are you a big fish in a little pond or a little fish in a big pond?" At the time he made that comment, I did not understand what he was asking me. By the way, I was the big fish.

The Egyptian Council covered a five-county area in southern Illinois. My boss made it very clear to me on my first day of work what my responsibilities were. I was to increase membership, raise money, recruit and train volunteers, plan programs, and direct the summer camp. Believe it or not, even after my job orientation of fire, I was anxious to get started. I didn't exactly know how or where to start. I just had to start somewhere.

Even though I was given no instruction as to how to complete those responsibilities, I still had the feeling that my boss would be more than willing to answer my questions and help me succeed. I liked the guy.

I took to this job. I spent many, many hours learning my new profession. I liked what the Boy Scouts stood for and still do. I was taking an active part in the shaping of young men into responsible adults. I had been a Boy Scout as a youth and enjoyed my time. I thought I should be able to rely on my boyhood experiences to help me with my new profession.

Since I was an executive for the Boy Scouts of

America, I knew that image was going to be important. I didn't smoke, drink, or cuss. I had a college degree and had recently left the military. I knew that I would have to associate with many levels of society, from the well off to those not so fortunate. The ability to communicate with people from all walks of life was a necessity. With my family, college, and military background, I could handle that.

The BSA required all new hires to go through a twenty-one-day training course in Texas. New hires went there after six months in the field. After six months, I boarded a local commuter plane in Carbondale to take me to the airport in St. Louis, Missouri, where I was to catch my flight to Dallas. By now, I was thirty years old, and this was the very first time I traveled on a plane by myself. I was going to spend twenty-one days in a foreign environment and have no one to rely on but myself. The seven years I spent in the military never provided me with that opportunity. This backwoods boy was about to learn that he could function on his own.

The training in Dallas was a great learning experience. I found out I could function with strangers outside my environment. I also discovered that I could do my job. There were new executives there from all across this country: New York City, Los Angeles, and Chicago. I had organized units and raised money as well as or better than most of them, and I was from a small district in southern Illinois. I was sure I was going to be okay in this new job.

I had been cruising along in my job as an exemplary

Boy Scout executive for about a year. I was having no problems being a role model. You know, clean living, hard work, the appearance of a good family life, etc. That year, my father-in-law invited me to a Cardinals baseball game with some of his friends. Although I didn't really know his friends, I knew I was going to have a good time. What American male wouldn't be able to enjoy male bonding at one of the most noble American pastimes?

My father-in-law, Richard, did the driving. He had a gold-colored Chrysler New Yorker. That thing was so long it would not fit in his garage. He had to build a new garage for it. He could transport seven people in it. And that is how many he was taking to the game.

It was a typical game. I don't remember who the Cardinals were playing, but we were all enjoying it. Of course, there was the traditional ritual of alcohol consumption (not by me; I am not a consumer of that type of beverage). A couple of our party had consumed a good deal of tradition during the game.

After the game was over, we loaded ourselves into the big gold Chrysler New Yorker and headed for home. But we didn't go straight home. Someone in our party had other ideas.

On the TV news the night before was a piece about a problem St. Louis was having with streetwalkers. These streetwalkers spent most of their time in a specific area of the city. Carleton, one member of our party, suggested we drive through that area and see what all the fuss was about. Carleton had also consumed a large amount of beer at the game. I was pretty sure he did not care what he was asking or even where he was. He just spoke what was currently on his mind.

I had no interest in seeing those ladies. I only wanted to get back to my father-in-law's house, pick up my family, and go home. I had to get up early the next day. I didn't speak my wishes. I was one of seven, and the majority of them were up for the trip. Majority rules. So Richard took the detour.

We were going into in an area known as a trouble spot to local police.

Our long, gold, expensive-looking Chrysler New Yorker was filled with adult men. More than one of them was beyond slightly inebriated.

It didn't take long before we recognized what we saw on the news as streetwalkers. The clothing was rather colorful, and their pants were skintight. The men in the car were quite intrigued. A longer look was needed, so Richard slowed his long, gold New Yorker way down, to about five miles per hour. Looking was the only intention.

The slower speed allowed us to make a better assessment of the previous night's news story. One young lady was wearing a shiny orange top and shiny purple pants. The top was loose fitting, and we all wondered if she used a shoehorn to get into those tight pants. The conclusion reached was unanimous. St. Louis had a problem on this street.

Suddenly, red lights were flashing behind us. Richard looked in his mirror to see what was going on. He pulled to the side of the road to let the police car pass. The problem was the police officer pulled in right behind him, parked his cruiser, got out, and started walking toward us. It was then we realized the police were really stopping us.

The two inebriated guys in the backseat scrunched down and tried to become invisible. The rest of us were trying to figure out what we did wrong. We were pretty sure we did nothing wrong. Having a couple of drunk guys in a car was not illegal. Richard, our driver, hadn't been drinking. We were clueless.

The cop approached our car and asked us what we were doing. Richard said, "We were at a Cardinals game, and we're heading home." The cop didn't buy it. I'm sure that officer was assessing his situation as a potential volatile problem. He probably felt he had to approach that suspect car, full of mature-looking white males, in an apprehensive manner, especially since the car was driving so slowly. The officer had to certainly question whether or not the car was going to stop and whether or not the men inside were planning to partake of the young lady's professional services. Being by himself, the officer had to be on high alert.

The policeman asked Richard why he was driving so slowly in this area.

Richard was honest with him. "We saw something on the news last night about this area. We were just looking. We had no intentions of stopping."

I guess the cop bought that, or perhaps he thought he scared us off. Anyway, he told us that because we were driving so slow in a car filled with men in that gold car, he just wanted to make sure we weren't up to no good. Talk about profiling.

You can bet we breathed a sigh of relief and made legal haste getting out of that area.

When that cop stopped us for what he believed was soliciting a known prostitute, I had a vision of a negative newspaper article. The title: "Local Scout executive arrested for prostitution." What a role model I would have become to the Scouts in my district.

When Richard and I got home and retold the adventure to our wives, they both made the same statement, which told us how much they understood our plight. "If we would have gotten a call to tell us we could pick you up at the police station, we would have told them to keep you there for the night. We'll be by in the morning." Some comfort they were.

Actually, they thought our adventure with the tight pants was funny. So do we. Now.

ZPG

In the summer of 1981, CJ informed me that our family was going to get larger. We were going to have another child. We were also about to achieve a goal we set for ourselves many years ago.

I remember the night we had our first sort-of-serious talk about our future together.

We were sitting in my car in her driveway chatting about the plans our friends had shared with us that night. They were engaged and making plans for their future. They told us they were planning on having kids, a big house to accommodate them, and lots of money to support them all. What young couple, serious about forever together, does not make those same plans?

CJ and I, to this point in our association, had not ever discussed anything resembling what our friends had shared with us that night. Like most young people together a lot, we made many unspoken implications of a long lasting relationship and nothing more.

Somehow the conversation that night turned to us speculating about what we wanted our families to look like. Both of us were in agreement. We wanted a big house and a big yard for our two children, just like our friends. One child was to be a son, the other a daughter, and they were going to come out in that order. We actually thought we had control over the order of arrival for our children. But young people know it all, don't they?

The house was going to have to be extremely large to accommodate our large dreams. There was no compromise. CJ said she wanted an indoor swimming pool with a sauna. She wanted horses out back in the barn. I was not going to be without my indoor racquetball court. Elvis was into racquetball, and I was into Elvis.

I think it is a pretty strong indication that a relationship has changed when a discussion about home and family happens in a car parked at the girlfriend's house. Ours certainly changed then and there.

The goodnight kiss felt different that night. The car was floating on air all the way home.

Nearly forty years later, we have long since given up our dream house. In fact, that youthful dream at our age now would require more energy than we could afford to expend. The dream about our children was one we happily managed to accomplish because of a college commitment.

When in college the two of us had decided to do our part toward ZPG (zero population growth). We were going to have only two children. That way, we could not be accused of increasing the population. In the sixties, maintaining ZPG was a big deal. Our college associates and we believed "having more than two children would add an undue burden onto an already over burdened world." Pretty philosophical, huh? Our twist to this theory was that we insisted we were going to have one boy and one girl in that order. We already had a son. We were quite pleased when we found out our new addition was going to be a girl.

I was in the service of the Boy Scouts when we found out we were adding on to the family. Although I enjoyed working for them, the income I earned was not extremely plentiful. Operational expenses were based on volunteer funding and program income. Southern Illinois in the early eighties was going through an economic slump. The program provided by the Scouts was great. Raising the funding for it was tough. In fact, the boss was so concerned about it that the professional staff was asked if they would voluntarily work only for expenses until we were able to raise sufficient funds to once again take a salary.

I was so much into the scouting program that I agreed. It would be about three months before I was able to draw a salary again.

I had to spend more time than normal working. My wife was pregnant and needed my help. Often I was not there to help her out.

Somehow CJ found a way to get us through that dreadful period.

We struggled for the next six months. I worked one hundred to 120 hours a week. I was a salaried worker, so the increase in work hours did nothing to increase my pay. The only money I was bringing home was my car allowance. It only paid for the gas I put in my car. As you can imagine, money was awfully tight. The life we had planned together while in college did nothing to prepare us for what we were experiencing right then.

Our new edition was going to arrive in February, prepared or not.

Brianna Paige, our ZPG child, decided to show up in the middle of a southern Illinois snowstorm.

Southern Illinois winters are unpredictable. They can be bitter cold, warm, rainy, or snowy. February 9 and 10, 1982, we had the worst snowstorm in anyone's recent memory. I do not believe I would be exaggerating if I said it snowed nearly ten inches over those two days. That was one of the very few times my boss told me not to go to the office.

CJ was due to deliver any day. In the middle of a snowstorm was not good timing, but it made no difference to our baby girl. She was ready to come out and play. She started knocking on her mommy's door with a great deal of emphasis around 8:00 a.m.

CJ told me it was time to go. She called her mother to have her meet us at the hospital, and I blazed a path to the car. It was still snowing when I put CJ and Richard in the car. Now all I had to do was drive to the hospital.

Usually it would take about thirty minutes to drive. The road crews were struggling to keep up with the snow, but the roads were at least passable. An hour later we pulled into the hospital's parking lot. CJ's parents were pulling in just ahead of us.

Their timing was perfect. They were in charge of Richard while CJ and I were in charge of birthing his sister.

A few minutes later, we were in the labor room. As soon as I entered, I started listening for screams coming from across the hall. I knew I was supposed to be attentive to my pregnant wife, but those screams of years ago have forever traumatized me. Even today, whenever I visit a labor room, I listen.

CJ's favorite soap was on the TV. One of the character's name was Brianna. CJ always liked the name, so we agreed to give our daughter the name of that character. During the show, the nurse came in and said she was going to get the doctor. The nurse was sure the baby was coming right then.

CJ disagreed. She was not going anywhere before her show was over.

My wife could be rather strong willed at times.

Perhaps our nurse was watching the same program because she entered our room just as the credits were rolling. CJ finally agreed to be wheeled into the delivery room and prepped for delivery.

I thought it took a long time for the doctor to get to the delivery room. He got caught up in his rounds or got caught up by a snowflake or two. I can't remember anymore. When he finally did arrive, he was in his suit and tie. I thought that was an odd outfit to wear while delivering a baby.

The attending nurse made some comment about his tie getting in the way. The doctor told her to pin his tie to his back. She agreed to take care of the tie. She grabbed a pair of scissors and cut it off. I'm sure she thought it would be faster to do that than to find a pin. The tie was no longer an issue.

Another issue was resolved in the delivery room. The nurse and my wife were having a dispute prior to Brianna's arrival. I affectionately referred to her as "Nurse Busy Body." I thought she took an entirely too active interest in everyone's personal lives. She certainly took an active interest in CJ's belly.

Nurse Busy Body was our Lamaze instructor. By the time we signed up for the class, CJ was nearing her due date. Nurse Busy Body immediately made the assessment. Because of the size of CJ's belly and Nurse Busy Body's many years as a pediatric nurse, CJ was having twins, absolutely no doubt about it. CJ told her we were having one big baby girl, and we had the pictures to prove it.

Nurse Busy Body refused to accept the evidence. The closer CJ got to her due date, the more insistent the nurse got that CJ was having twins despite what sonograms indicated. My wife knew she was having a big baby, not twins.

When Nurse Busy Body found out CJ was delivering, she insisted on being in the delivery room to prove she was right.

I swear, when Brianna came out, the nurse wanted the doctor to root around for the twin. Obviously, the nurse was wrong, and CJ was right.

The snow was still on the ground when we took Brianna home.

Our family was now complete. We reached ZPG. We had a boy and a girl and in that order.

Murphy's Army

I was born with an *X* on my back. I learned that at an early age. I was never able to get away with anything. I have siblings who appear not to have the same *X* handicap as me. Living with that target on my back is just part of my life, so I try very hard to walk the straight and narrow path.

Whenever I venture off, I will get caught. If the speed limit is sixty-five miles per hour, the police will pull me over for driving sixty-eight miles per hour, even if I get passed by some jerk driving eighty-five miles per hour. I know that, so I might as well drive the speed limit.

I don't tell little white lies (or big fat ones for that matter) to my wife. Somehow, I do something that lets her know I lied to her. As every man knows, women can be vicious when they feel they have been wronged. Those consequences are too scary to think about.

The *X* on my back may explain why Murphy visited me in full force one summer. You know, Murphy's Law. If anything can go wrong, it will.

I was not looking for him, nor was I prepared for him. This guy came unannounced and uninvited. His timing was bad. I was a Boy Scout camp director when Mr. Murphy came to see me in the summer of 1985. He came during staff week and stayed a while longer.

The purpose of staff week is to ensure the camp is ready for the onslaught of campers. Campsites need to be prepared. Food needs to be purchased and stored; the staff has to be trained. The swimming pool has to be filled. The boats need to be taken to the lakefront. The grass has to be mowed. The parking lot has to be cleaned of debris. There are at least a hundred other things to do to ensure scouts have a fun and safe week at camp.

My full-time job was as a professional Boy Scout executive. My boss gave me the additional assignment as camp director that year. I did not mind it too much. In fact, I welcomed the challenge. I enjoyed the program aspect of my Boy Scout profession. I thought, *The boss must like me if he gave me the assignment. Bring it on. I'm ready. I can handle it.*

I managed to complete all the prep work without incident. The boss was quite pleased with how easily I completed the challenging task. He was looking forward to visiting the camp at some point during the summer. The boss told me he would be able to come and not have to worry about anything. The boss expected to only have fun. I intended for that to happen.

The first three days were relatively uneventful. The staff members arrived, and introductions were made. Each staff counselor got his assignment, and training was underway. We were having a good time.

On the fourth day, three days before scouts were to arrive, Mr. Murphy sent one of his lieutenants to my camp to start his invasion. I was enjoying my morning coffee when I saw the aquatics director amble toward the dining hall. Ben Jackson never ambled. He was a tall, lanky kid who was always in a hurry. There was no one with him, but he seemed to be having a conversation with somebody. I could tell by his appearance that he was extremely flustered, worried, and angry. This kid was only about twenty-five years old and quite mature for his age. I didn't think a young kid could actually show that type of emotion. So I was worried.

Ben reminded me that camp opened in three days (as if I didn't know that). He said, "Pete, first of all, I want you to know I'm doing the best I can. I did everything I'm s'pposed to do, and I did it right. I don't have any idea how it happened." All these excuses were flowing from his mouth. "All right, Ben, calm down," I said. "What are you trying to tell me?"

"Pete, I started filling up the swimming pool two days ago. It should be full by now. It isn't. The water seems to be going in. The pool's about three-quarters full, and the water's not getting any deeper. I worked here last year, and by now the swimming pool was completely full. I don't know what's wrong."

I went with Ben to the swimming pool, and sure enough, he was right. We had a big problem. In three days, the campers would be here. Not having a pool was a huge problem.

There didn't seem to be any leaks. The ground around the pool was dry. An initial check of the pool did not turn up any cracks that I could see. Draining the pool did not seem feasible at this point.

It turned out to be the pump feeding water to the pool.

It was a very old pump and needed to be replaced, but this was a Boy Scout camp. It ran on a tight budget. A way was found to make a temporary patch that hopefully would allow the pump to get it through this season.

Because of the patch, the pump could not handle its usual volume of water. It would take longer to fill the pool. The scouts were still going to be here before the pool water was to its safe capacity. We would have to use the boating area for a while. Though I figured out a safe boating and swimming schedule, I had nightmares of Scouts crashing into each other on the beach.

With that crisis averted, I could breathe easy.

Or so I thought.

Mr. Murphy, apparently, must have thought I would be his next big challenge, because on Wednesday of the first week of camp, he decided to bring his whole army.

Of course, that would be the same day my boss came for a visit. The invasion began at sunrise.

Every Wednesday at sunrise was our mile swim. In past years we would have nearly fifty scouts participate in the swim. This year was no exception. Because of the number of participants, we used the lake. The year before, I ran the mile swim, so I knew the routine well. This year, I planned to watch it from the camp director's perspective. All I was going to do was watch, socialize with the campers, and evaluate the aquatic staff's performance. That was my plan. Murphy had another plan for me.

Although it was late June, the morning was damp from the previous night's rain. The sun had not risen enough to warm the air. It was still chilly, so I decided to wear my bright yellow jacket. What a fashion statement I was making: red ball cap on my head, bright yellow jacket over a green scout uniform shirt, green uniform shorts with matching green knee socks, the green tassels, barely tanned legs, and white tennis shoes. Although the sun could not yet be seen, the horizon was engulfed in orange. It was quite a contrast of colors for the early morning risers to wake up to. It was a beautiful morning.

Ben approached me and told me that one of his staff was in bed sick, so he was shorthanded. He asked me if I could help him since I knew how the swim worked. Of course, I had no problems helping him out. What are camp directors for if not to help out?

The year before, I always walked along the boat dock while the swimmers would swim by, and that is what I would do this year. So I grabbed my rescue pole and took my place on the dock. I had walked up and down that dock so much the year before that I did not even have to look down at the dock. I was sure I could do it with my eyes closed.

I was way too confident. I couldn't see him, but Murphy was right beside me as I walked up and down the dock, alongside each swimmer, rescue pole in hand. He waited about thirty minutes before he struck. At his appointed time, it happened. I, for some reason, decided to look at my feet. What happened next could have been on *America's Funniest Home Videos*.

The following is a reenactment of what I know actually happened. You could talk to other Scouts who were there, and they may tell you something different. This is my story, and I am sticking to it.

When I looked down at my feet, no dock was under them, only water. Apparently, I had walked about three to four feet past the dock. When I finally realized where I was, I tried to get to back to the dock. I'm sure I looked like a cartoon character at that moment to the others on the beach. I had to get back to the dock. I did not want to be the source of a scout leader's funny summer camp story.

For what seemed like several seconds, my feet started running for the dock. Just as the tip of my right foot touched it, *kerplop*! I fell into the water feet first and sank below the surface. I resurfaced spitting out water, climbed back onto the dock, called to a watching scout leader, and handed him my pole. I squished off the dock and headed to my cabin to change clothes. There was no denying it now. I was going to be the talk of the camp.

The leaders' meeting would be an hour from now. At least that gave a little time to prepare for the onslaught of razzing now on the agenda.

I was standing on the front porch of the dining hall waiting for the men to arrive. I was ready for their razzing. After a couple of minutes, I said, "All right. Let's grab a chair and sit out here on the porch." I grabbed mine and proceeded to set three of the four legs on the edge of the pouch. You guessed it; over I went, backwards onto the grass.

This day was not shaping up to be very pretty. Getting through that meeting was another challenge.

Just as the meeting was ending, my boss drove up, and right behind him came Bill, my commissary clerk, who needed to see me. I spent a few minutes updating my boss on how well camp was going so far. I had previously briefed him on the swimming pool problem. Of course, I left out the information about my morning swim and my feeble attempt at lawn care. There would be plenty of people to tell those stories anyway. I needed to visit with my commissary clerk.

We were going to issue out cold cuts and bread to the campers that day for lunch. We had plenty of food when camp opened, but something had just happened to the bread. I was absolutely sure I ordered plenty. Murphy had to feed his army, I guess. We had nowhere near enough loaves of bread for lunch. So I decided to get into my Subaru station wagon and head into town. I invited the boss along. We could talk about business along the way. There was plenty of time.

Murphy was on the attack again. The front tire of my wagon was flat. No problem. I'd change it. Problem: my spare was flat.

For some reason, Mr. Boss Man found this extremely amusing. He was going to be gracious, though, and drive me into town in his car. Boss Man was extremely attached to his car. His car was a 1982 candy-apple red Oldsmobile Cutlass Supreme with all the extras. He said he was unhappy because it was a leased car and it had to be turned in the next day.

Quite frankly, I was surprised he drove it to camp. The road was usually dusty, and the car rarely had a speck of dust on it. I was doubly surprised when he offered to use his car to transport the needed bread.

As we were driving into town, we both thought we heard a strange noise coming from the front end of his car. It was for just a split second. We didn't feel anything, so we kept driving. When I heard that noise, I was a little apprehensive. So many unforeseen things had already happened. By now I was a little gun shy.

We arrived without incident at the store where we shopped for camp supplies. I was thankful nothing out of the ordinary had happened yet. We loaded the bread. It was time to go back to camp. As I opened the door to get in, Murphy made sure I saw the front end of Boss Man's car. It was then I realized what that noise was. I told my boss that we lost one of his hubcaps.

This was the very same leased car he planned to turn in tomorrow. How was he going to explain the missing hubcap? And would he possibly make me pay for it? He had an expensive car. This would cost me a lot of money. I thought sure he was going to be mad.

Fortunately, he wasn't. He said we would stop where we thought we heard the noise and try to find his hubcap. I think Mr. Murphy slipped up on this one because we found that missing hubcap. There wasn't even so much as a ding on it. We arrived back at camp without further incident. The campers never even knew of the possible catastrophe.

Murphy's Army had one more try at disrupting my life.

Just before supper, a new scoutmaster of one of our

newest troops told me that half of his campers were absolutely adamant about going home. They could not stand to spend any more time here. They were miserable, and no amount of persuasion on his part would change their mind.

I gathered up a bunch of seasoned scoutmasters, and we all went to see these Scouts. All the boys in the troop were from an inner-city unit. There was not a single boy among them who had ever been in the woods before, let alone out of the city. The boys were extremely worried about all those strange noises they heard at night. The bugs were bothersome as well. They were hungry. Their brand new leader, although very enthusiastic, was having a difficult time instructing the boys how to cook over an open fire. The previous day's rain only added to these scouts' determination to leave.

It is a beautiful thing to watch caring men in action. I knew they would be able to say the right things. These young men finished out the week. Every single one of them told me how he appreciated being given the opportunity to stay the entire week. They had a great time.

I woke up the next morning, and Murphy was gone. I know this because the rest of the summer was smooth sailing.

Although that was one of the most difficult few weeks of my entire life, it was probably the most rewarding experience I have ever had. I found out what kind of stuff I was made of. I am pretty sure I can handle just about anything now.

Thinking back on it now, all that stuff really was funny.

The skills I learned in the army and the Boy Scouts would be put into use in my third career. At age forty-two, I would finally become a teacher. It is that career in which I have spent the bulk of my working life and the one from which I will retire.

The IDOC Physical

During my adult life, I have taken two physicals required for entry into a job. The first was for the army, and the second was for employment with the Illinois Department of Corrections. I have previously explained my army physical. The IDOC provided me with a second memorable experience exposing my character.

The army physical was one in which I willingly participated. I was a reluctant participant in the Illinois Department of Corrections physical.

I was twenty-three, unemployed, and graduating from college when I entered the military. I was not capable of supporting myself at that time. My path had been predetermined by the government. Since I did not consider being a disloyal citizen, I had no other choice than to go into the army. I was not responsible enough to make a career decision, so having someone else make that decision for me was certainly a comfortable feeling.

Twenty years later, in 1992, I was once again unemployed. But this time circumstances were much different. At age forty-two I could not rely on governmental intervention. I alone was totally responsible for what was about to happen. I could not afford to be careless about it. I was married with children. What I decided not only affected me but also my family. Any decision could not be taken lightly.

Obviously, I did decide to take that IDOC physical, but there were many forces pulling me to participate in that physical despite desires to the contrary.

In 1988, after eight years, I resigned as an executive for the Boy Scouts of America. The next four years were spent searching for a worthwhile career. I was always looking for something that would not be below my self-inflated status as a member of the Russey family. My parents were both optometrists. All my siblings were very respectfully employed. I could not let them down. That was a great deal of pressure I imposed on myself.

My wife, on the other hand, was much more grounded. She was constantly engaged in battle with my inflated ego. She kept reminding me that although the status in family blood is important, it is the family I live with and am responsible for that is the absolute most important thing in my life. Thank God for CJ. In spite of my wife's effort, I spent those four years unsuccessfully trying to inflate my ego.

The first journey toward full-time employment was with an international multibillion dollar company. I left my family in Missouri to sell janitorial supplies for the company in southern Illinois. I moved in with my parents. While living with them, my mother passed away. I also discovered I was not as well suited for this job as I thought I would be. I lasted about two months. Thirty dollars short of being able to draw unemployment, that multibillion dollar international company decided to let me go.

I moved back home to continue my search. Three months later, I was being interviewed for a prospective job when my father-in-law's phone call interrupted the interview. He informed me that my father had just died. More bad news, which meant immediate employment was, once again, put on hold. I had been named executor, along with my brother, of my parents' will. That business needed to be tended to.

A couple months later, I moved my family to southern Illinois after being employed by a local hospital. I was hired to be the Director of Volunteer Services. The work I did in the Boy Scouts made me a shoe-in for this job. Like the Boy Scouts, it was not the best paying job, but they made me carry a pager on my belt. This was 1990, before the onslaught of the cell phone. Back then, I thought only "big shots" wore pagers. I was impressed with myself. I wasn't highly paid, but I had suddenly become elevated to the status of big shot, at least in my own mind. This job, I felt, befitted my ego but only lasted about six months because I was offered a better paying job with my hometown hospital.

My hometown hospital allowed me to put another impressive title on my résumé, the Director of Special Projects. I was to be the very first person to fill the position. It was to be a public relations/marketing position. I did public relations and marketing for the Scouts my entire career with them. I was suited for this job. The hospital administrator even told me he expected to eventually make me a vice president. Talk about a boost to the ego! Things were finally starting to look up. Three months later, he had a change of heart and decided to let me go. All he said was that after thinking about it more, I did not fit into his plans for the hospital. There really are people like that in this world. I had moved my family for this job and once again felt as if I let them down.

I could not understand why all this was happening to me. I wanted to work. I needed to work. I kept thinking of my dad and believed he would be disappointed with me. How could I be of value without work? This was a very difficult period for me and my family. Thinking back on it now, I was meant to go through this. I was being led.

My ego was substantially deflated. The family was depending on me to take care of them. Time to draw on unemployment again to ensure food could be put on the table. I wound up working in a mall warehouse part-time, unloading trucks. I also did some substitute teaching in several schools and continued looking for a career suitable for my lofty status.

My wife and her family, several times during this period, suggested I work for the Illinois Department of Corrections. There were jobs available, and it represented good solid work. I, of course, would hear nothing of it. Functioning in an environment where I would be locked up while working, I felt, would be beneath me. Criminals are locked up, not upstanding members of society. I certainly was an upstanding member of society.

One day, CJ told me that the Illinois Department of Corrections was having an open job interview. She strongly suggested I attend. Her father agreed. There was no way I was going to work for them. But just to get my wife and her family off my back, I agreed to go interview. When I didn't get hired, at least I wouldn't have to hear them squawk about it anymore.

I discovered that two other men in my community were interested in the IDOC interview. One was an unemployed coal miner. The other, my wife's brother, owned a business but was considering selling it. I drove them and myself to the interview site. They were looking forward to passing the interview and being hired. I was hoping I would not pass.

The interview was a day-long event. It would be divided into three activities. A physical was the first activity. At forty-two years of age, I was not sure of my ability to physically compete with men and women many years my junior. Evidently, I was in decent shape. I passed the physical.

The results of the first two activities were made known to each applicant before proceeding to the next. The coal miner was unable to pass the physical. He was done. The next step was a series of mental aptitude tests. These tests, for me, were not difficult. I passed them as well.

Taking the IDOC physical made me painfully aware that I was no longer a young man. Although I did struggle somewhat with the physical test, it was during the written exam I was reminded that my age was advancing.

My brother-in-law and I had finished the exam and were having a pleasant conversation in the hallway. A young man walked up to me and asked me if I recognized him. I looked up at him and told him I did not. He reminded me that he was the camp staffer who threw the tent pole through my station wagon front window while taking down summer camp twelve years earlier.

I still didn't recognize him. The Scout this kid was talking about was a fourteen-year-old scrawny, little, skinny kid, short in stature. The young man standing in front of me was well over six feet tall and stocky. That was certainly a rude awakening, and I told that kid so. We all laughed about it. I have not seen that kid since.

The last test of the day was an interview. My brother-in-law and I were now being interviewed. Because I didn't really care if I passed, I really had no clue how I would handle the interview. But my ego would not let me intentionally fail. I had no knowledge about that type of employment. I answered all their questions the best I could. Those that made it to the interview process would be informed in about two weeks if they passed, and from those, several would be offered a job. My wife's brother decided to keep his business. The government once again made my career choice.

I had spent my entire adult life working with the ability to freely move from location to location. The absolute last thing I wanted was to work locked behind a fence. Yet life once more had another plan for me. I was going to work behind a fence.

I started my corrections career as a prison guard. My objective, though, was to become a teacher at the prison where I worked. It was newly opened and had teaching positions available. I had applied for one of them before becoming a prison guard. I told CJ if I were still in the uniform after six months I would leave corrections to look for something else. CJ did not like it, but she humored me.

I woke up on April 3, 1993, and realized it was six months to the day as a guard for IDOC. Before I left for work that day, I said to CJ, "It's been six months to the day. If I don't get a call today, I'm leaving." I walked out the door and left for work. About an hour into my workday, the school principal saw me and said he was planning to call me later in the day. He was going to invite me to be interviewed for one of his empty teaching spots. He asked right there if I would like to schedule an interview.

One month later, I was given the opportunity to do what I was trained to do in college. I became a teacher within the system. Now I have the responsibility to provide inmates with the tools needed to prevent them from returning to prison after being released into society.

It has been over sixteen years since I took that physical, and I am still employed with the Illinois Department of Corrections. I can honestly say this has been a good career choice.

The Spanish Invasion

When my daughter, Brianna, was in the eleventh grade, she and several of her friends went on a class trip to Spain. Their Spanish language teacher, Andrew Peters, had vacationed in Spain a couple of times. He convinced the school to allow him to organize a class trip to Spain. His trip was available to any of his Spanish language students with a desire to go.

Andrew was a young man not too far from his college graduation. He had a genuine thirst to deal with the ever-changing attitude of the teenager. That is a requirement of every high school teacher. This trip was either going to forever quench his thirst or make him thirstier.

His Spanish students brought a flyer home announcing the trip. I think CJ and I were more excited about the possibility of the trip than our daughter. Many of Brianna's friends expressed an interest in going. Brianna's interest, I believe, was based solely on her peers' interest, not on any deep-seated desire to go to a foreign country.

In retrospect, I am pretty sure they all decided to go because it would get them out of their boring little town. They did not really understand or care for the opportunity about to be handed to them.

Sending a child on a class trip presents serious challenges to any parent. It does not matter whether it is across the state or across the world. Money, of course, is a major challenge. It always seems that with opportunities of this magnitude, volunteers will be needed. With busy people, like my wife and me, allocating volunteer time for planning is a problem.

The three of us attended the informational meeting. Brianna was adamant about going to Spain with her friends. Although we were excited about the prospect, CJ and I had some reluctance about letting her go. Did we have the money? It would take some hardship, but we could manage it.

As big a challenge as the money was, we were more concerned about Brianna's commitment to the trip. She and her friends tended to be prima donnas and very close. If her friends backed out after we committed money, would Brianna still want to go? We would make her go anyway, but if her friends were not with her, she could decide not to enjoy the experience. Fortunately, that was a moot point.

Brianna assured us she and her friends were going to Spain. Mother and Father made arrangements to pay for the trip and then were promptly recruited by Andrew to be the co-chairs of the newly formed Spanish Travelers.

Fund-raisers were planned and volunteers recruited. It is kind of funny, though; teenagers don't seem to give much thought to how things they want are paid for. At least that was the impression we got from our group of young people. Often, something of critical importance to their world would magically "come up" when they were scheduled to work at a fund-raiser. It was a good thing the Spanish Travelers were blessed with a great group of adult volunteers. They would somehow ensure their Spanish Travelers' responsibility was covered.

In addition to the many fund-raisers Andrew's students were to take part in, they were also responsible for at least one written report on a famous Spanish person. My daughter chose to write about a well-known actress, Salma Hayek. Brianna asked me to help her gather information and pictures about Ms. Hayek. Thank God for the Internet. I didn't know much about Ms. Hayek, but I did know how to use the Internet.

In 1998, our server was very, very sluggish. Once a picture of her was found, all we had to do was watch as the image would reveal itself. The image would start at the top of the screen. We saw hair. The image slid down a little more. Now we could see a pair of eyes. A little farther down, and now we saw a chin. The image was only half revealed. It was definitely Salma. Now we saw a pair of bare shoulders.

Brianna and I were both thinking, *Could it be?* A few seconds later, we were concerned about what the downloading image was going to reveal to us. We clicked out of the site. Today, the image would just pop up. We would not have the luxury of clicking out of the picture before it's too late.

Andrew and I spent many nights before and after the committee meeting developing plans for the trip to Spain. At one of those meetings, Andrew made me an offer I couldn't refuse. He told me that because of the number of kids we had signed up, we needed to have one more adult chaperone. Andrew wanted me to be that chaperone. He told me the trip would cost me 150 dollars, plus my expenses.

How could anyone refuse an offer like that? I accepted it with my wife's blessing, but not Brianna's. She was convinced Dad was going on the trip to spy on her. And there probably was a little truth to that. As for me, this common man from a small southern Illinois hick town was making plans to go to Europe and basically go for free.

The trip was to last seventeen days. We were to visit four cities, beginning with a three-day stay on the Mediterranean Sea and ending with a four-day stay in Madrid. Of course, the beaches of the Mediterranean were the most appealing to our young adults and probably the reason the trip was attractive to them in the first place. The boys must have been thinking about those European girls. The girls were probably dreaming about the European boys. The best place for American boys and girls to see those European beauties was at the beach on the Mediterranean.

Andrew and I were going to invade Spain with a group of nineteen people. The Spanish Travelers were lucky enough to have the family of one of our group and another teacher accompany us while we traversed Spain. Responsible adults are always a good thing when hosting teenagers.

Plans were in place. Our bags were packed. A caravan of parents and travelers headed for Lambert International Airport in St. Louis.

Ready or not, Spain was about to be invaded.

But first, there was the adventure of boarding travelers and luggage onto a commuter train that was to take us to the airport.

Nineteen passengers and luggage can certainly take up a large amount of train space. It was a good thing we boarded after rush hour.

I know we were a strange sight to the well-traveled eye. There was no way to hide our backwoodsness. We were from a small southern Illinois town. Many of us had never been on an airplane, let alone flown on one over this continent, across an ocean, and into an entirely different continent.

Some in our group were natural born adventurers. Ensuring that they got on the same train as the group and didn't venture off on their own was the first big challenge. Andrew and I knew we were going to have our hands full.

So much happened on this trip—most of it planned. But chaperoning a bunch of teenagers meant unplanned things were going to happen. It was the job of Andrew and I to be prepared for all of it.

It sure is funny what one remembers after the passage of time. I am sure what I remember is not necessarily what my daughter remembers. The following are just short synopses of the things that still stick out in my mind many years later.

The first leg of the trip was to fly to New York, where we would make a connecting flight to Madrid, Spain.

The LaGuardia Airport, New York, USA, is where we landed. New York is "my kind of town." At least that is what the song says. I really wouldn't know if it is true. This common man from a small southern Illinois town has not done much airplane traveling. All I saw of New York was the airport. New York looked just like a regular indoor shopping mall to me. Just different names on the storefronts.

The trip from New York to Madrid was surprisingly uneventful. I do, though, remember one specific conversation two attractive young women were having behind Andrew and me. I don't make a habit of listening in to other people's conversations, but I heard one of them say "Madrid," so I had to tune in. Maybe I would gain some valuable information I could use later.

These two had just graduated from college and were talking about what they were going to do. They met for the first time on the plane. One was going to Europe on a scholarship to continue her graduate studies. The other was given money for graduation. She chose to spend her graduation money in Madrid, Spain.

I was truly fascinated by that young lady's adventurous spirit. You see, she knew no one in Madrid and had no specific plans. She intended to visit there completely on her own. I was jealous of her youthful exuberance. Andrew thought she was a nutcase. I never saw her again after we landed in Madrid. I still wonder how she made out.

About eight hours later, the Spanish Travelers successfully landed in Spain. To our kids, the invasion was not going to officially start until we arrived at the beaches on the Mediterranean. First, we had to meet up with Manuel. He was to be our tour guide for the entire trip across Spain. Manuel, now, that is a Spanish-sounding name. And he looked the part too. Some of the young ladies in our group might describe him this way. Tall, dark, handsome, early thirties, Antonio Banderas look-a-like. Needless to say, he was quite a hit with them. Where he led, they would follow.

Manuel led our group to the far end of the Madrid Airport and boarded with us onto a shuttle plane that would take us to those beaches at Fuengirola, Spain. We could feel the excitement building.

Little did we know our plane would be stranded on the landing strip for over an hour. No information was forthcoming to us about why. All kinds of bad stuff creep into the unprepared teenage brain. Andrew and I, who also didn't know what was happening, spent a good part of that layover in combat with those creepy brains.

We finally got underway and landed without incident at Fuengirola. Manuel later told us that Madrid Airport was having to handle a situation with Spanish terrorists. In 1998, *terrorist* was not as terrifying a word as it is today, so we didn't think much more about it.

On the hour-long shuttle bus ride from the small airport to our hotel, Manuel explained to our group of travelers what they were about to experience in his homeland. Looking out the bus windows, we could see the sandy beaches, a bright cloudless sky, and the Mediterranean. The kids' enthusiasm could hardly be contained.

Although we didn't express it to each other, I know Andrew and I did have a small concern. We were in Europe. Right or wrong, many Americans, I believe, are under the impression that most European beachgoers have a different idea of what appropriate beach attire is. Manuel must have sensed that. He assured us that we would not be going near any nude beaches. Dealing with parents about that matter would not be pleasant.

Manuel was not exactly honest with us.

Our hotel was literally on one of the beautiful Mediterranean beaches. The hotel and sandy beaches should have taken my breath away, but there was not time to admire the scenery. Andrew and I had to get those teenagers into their rooms before they got lost from their luggage. I think, if left alone, they would have headed straight for the beaches with no thought of changing into swimsuits. We managed to get them checked into their rooms. Mission accomplished.

Andrew and I located our rooms and began settling in. While Andrew was unpacking his bags, I grabbed my camcorder and started filming the awesome sights around us. Our room was on the tenth floor. That afforded me the opportunity to look down over the city. It was impressive to see. As I looked out my window to the left, I saw groups of tightly packed buildings stretching for what seemed liked several miles. In those groups I could make out churches, other hotels, stores, and homes that appeared to be mansions. The side streets were very small. I was sure if two cars met going in opposite directions they would exchange paint jobs. No matter where we went in Spain, every side street I saw appeared that way.

Straight ahead and to my right as far as I could see was the beach and the crystal blue waters of the ocean. When I zoomed way out, I could make out what looked to be huge cargo ships.

It had only been probably thirty minutes since we checked in. Andrew and I were sure some of our group had already hit the beach. I began scanning it with my camera.

On one of my scans over the beach, I noticed a boy about five running out of the water into the arms of his mother. *A nice family beach,* I thought. *Wait a minute! That lady doesn't have a top on.*

"Andy, I think we have a problem!"

I gave Andrew my camera so he could verify what I saw. He did. What were we to do? What were we going to tell the parents? Manuel assured us we wouldn't have to deal with this. No, wait. He said no nude beaches. He didn't say anything about topless.

The kids were probably already on the beach. Andrew and I were sure that some of the kids had already seen what we just did. Nothing could be done about that. We finally decided not to make a big deal out of it. If the kids told us about it, we would handle it then. Nothing was ever said.

We spent three days on the Mediterranean. The guys saw European girls in bikinis, and the girls saw sun-baked, handsome, young beach boys. On the fourth day, we moved our invasion to the north.

One of the next stops was Granada. Manuel told

us that our bus was going to be greeted by some of the locals. They were gypsies, and the ones I saw looked the way I imagined a gypsy would look. Men and women wore earrings. The women's were large and dangly. I remember the large, clinking gold bracelets the women wore on their wrists. All the gypsies wore loose-fitting colorful clothes. Our guide told us we needed to be careful. Manuel emphatically told all of us not to speak to them. Their goal was to part us from our belongings. The warning was not heeded by everyone.

Nancy had no sooner gotten off the bus when a gypsy cornered her. Nancy was the most outgoing and adventurous of our group. I guess it didn't help when Nancy started pointing and taking pictures of one of the gypsies. Nancy even waved at the gypsy she was photographing. The lady gypsy took that as an invitation to make Nancy the target of her philandering. Nancy's friends were trying to convince the gypsy to move on when Andrew finally intervened. The gypsy left. This would not be the last time we would be challenged by Nancy's adventuresome spirit.

Later in the evening, the Spanish Travelers were going to have the opportunity to experience a flamenco dance at the downtown stage theater. Andrew considered this to be the highlight of the trip, and it was to be the most formal event of our travels. Nice clothes were mandatory. Andrew took the time and carefully hung his up in the closet the night before. When he went to put them on, there was a problem. His shirt was wrinkled.

I made a comment about the shirt. Apparently a wrinkled shirt was nothing new to Andrew. He came prepared for just such a thing. He put on his shirt and picked up the portable iron he had been heating up. Yep! Our leader was about to iron his shirt while he was wearing it. I remember saying to him, "This is going to be amusing." How he kept from burning himself, I will never know.

I have to admit, though, I was a little disappointed. I thought it would be amusing to see Andrew give me a prequel to the flamenco, as his shirt got a little too warm. I mean, what would you expect when you see someone iron a shirt while wearing it?

The kids were not as eager as Andrew and I to see an authentic flamenco. The dance was to be performed by a nationally renowned dance team. There must have been over twenty in the dance team.

What I remember the most, though, is the featured dancer. I thought he would be younger than he looked. He was probably in his late thirties. He did have a slim build, as I expected, and muscular legs, of course. He wore a bright red shirt and black pants. I remember the taps on his shoes clicking across the floor. I thought he looked more like a farmer to me than a dancer. That guy sure could dance a great flamenco. My seat was so close to the stage that I not only saw the dancer's sweat, but I also was hit by beads of it. It would be safe to say I was mesmerized by his dancing. I was in awe of the dancer, sweat and all.

We loaded the bus and moved on to another town the next day.

In Segovia I was once again awestruck. I actually touched the Roman aqueduct. The structure in Segovia was over 2,900 feet long. The part I observed had a series of two tiered arches towering over one hundred feet above my head. They sort of looked like McDonald's arches stacked one on top of the other. Here is a massive piece of architecture spanning several countries and still in existence after two thousand years.

I remember suddenly being fascinated by contrast. Spain was full of buildings many centuries or even millenniums old. Most of them were still in perfect condition and being used every day. What history and traditions these buildings must contain!

In America we are obsessed with new. Here, many forty-year-old stadiums or school buildings are considered obsolete and must be torn down. Busch Stadium in St. Louis was about forty years old when it was torn down and replaced with a new stadium. I was fortunate enough to watch Bob Gibson and Sandy Koufax pitch against each other in that stadium. Talk about a history. We do not have the history of the rest of the world, but after visiting Spain, I wonder why we don't find our history as imperative to retain.

I saw my responsibility with the Spanish Travelers as a threefold assignment. I was to assist Andrew in watching over the group. I was to stay out of my daughter's way so she could enjoy her trip. Most importantly, I was to personally watch over her as inconspicuously as possible.

Her mother and I had talked at length about this.

She told me to be discreet while watching her. CJ said, "Leave her alone, and Brianna will come to you when she needs something." I knew that was sound advice. I was equipped to assure Brianna would have a good time, and now so could I. My personal goal while taking in the sights of Spain with my daughter was to allow her to have fun without her feeling I was being obtrusive. It was in Segovia that Brianna found out a father's true value.

While I was observing the architectural wonders of the Roman aqueduct, Brianna was observing the wonders of a local department store. She found something not quite in her budget and just had to have it. It didn't matter what it was. This was the first time on our trip she acknowledged I was with her. I was just so grateful she finally realized her dad had some use after all. Mom was right. Brianna did come to me.

After leaving the architectural phenomenon of Segovia, our bus headed toward Madrid. We were to spend our last four days in that city.

While driving into Madrid, Manuel was very clear about which part of city we were to stay away from. We were going to stay near the downtown district. Manuel told us that part of the city was laid out like the spokes of a wheel. He said, "As long as you stay to the right, you will be okay. If you are unfortunate enough to take a wrong spoke, you could wind up in the seedy part of the city." No one really paid any attention to that piece of information. We were with Andrew, and he was familiar with Madrid. Also, we had faith that our tour guide would not lead us astray.

I am not a fan of Madrid, Spain. To me it will always be dirty and somewhat lacking in morals. My opinion may change someday if ever given the opportunity to visit again.

Our travel agent informed us that our room accommodations in Madrid would be in a five-star hotel. Every one of us swears he was wrong. The Spanish Travelers refer to it as Bates Hotel. Our hotel had holes in the hallway wall where telephones had been. It was as if some strange unseen force yanked them out in a fit of rage. The room Andrew and I stayed in had a missing ceiling fan. The wires were still exposed. Perhaps that same unseen force pulled out our fan. We also had infrequent hot water. The walls appeared to be paper thin, and the food was lousy. The rest of the travelers had similar reports.

Several members of the Travelers had seen the movie *Psycho*. Those of you who have seen the movie know Bates Motel has a prominent part in the horror movie. Staying in Bates Hotel for four nights was going to provide some of us with stories of bravery to be passed down to our ancestors.

After checking into Bates Hotel, Andrew assembled our group of invaders. He planned to take our group to Puerta del Sol, a major hub of activity in downtown Madrid, to see a Spanish festival. To get there, we were to walk through one of Madrid's public parks. Andrew and I were escorting our group of teenagers through that park when we all saw some disgusting things. Trash littered the ground. It looked as if men and women were openly having sex. Someone pulled down his or her (I am still not sure which) pants and defecated on the ground not ten feet from us. What an impression Madrid was making on our young!

Something was always going on at Puerta del Sol. We took advantage of many of them. On one of our trips there, I somehow got lost. I think I was taking pictures, and when I turned around, the group was gone.

Everyone was to meet at Puerta del Sol in the event of a lost traveler. We all knew the way. Evidently, I forgot the way. I took a wrong spoke.

There I was, a responsible adult, lost in a big city. I spent over twenty years in the Boy Scouting program as a youth and adult and seven years in the army. Surely, I could handle this. One major problem: not a single soul I came across could speak my language. Every street I turned down looked dirtier than the last.

I remembered Manuel warning us not to go to the east. That was where all the bad guys hung out, and I believed I looked like I was presenting myself as an easy target. I was walking around in shorts, a camera bag over my shoulder, and a straw hat on my head. It was not looking too good for little ol' Pete.

I turned down another street and saw a bunch of tables and chairs. They were part of a restaurant. The people looked friendly. I walked into the restaurant and up to the bar. While trying to explain my plight, the only Spanish I knew was Puerta del Sol, which I kept saying over and over.

Someone finally understood my plight and

decided to draw me a map. It didn't help. The map did not make sense to me. The guy took me outside and pointed to a street sign and then to where he drew in Puerta del Sol on the map. Now I understood why I could not read the map. Where I was going was in the center of the map, and my current location was on the outside edge of the map. The map was backwards from the way I would have drawn it.

Eventually, I made it back to the group safe and sound. Some adult example I set for the group. I can't remember ever being as afraid as I was that day. I might as well have been dropped off in some foreign country without the ability to communicate. Oh, wait a minute. That's what happened.

During the entire trip through Spain, there was a mystery I tried to solve. Everywhere we went, hot dogs were served for breakfast. I have never and still don't consider hot dogs breakfast food. This mystery was finally solved the last night of our stay in Spain. One of our travelers had a sausage pizza delivered to his room. It was loaded with sliced hot dogs.

The previous sixteen days we spent in Spain were eventful. On the seventeenth day we were all ready to go home. Getting the kids loaded up for the short trip to the airport was no problem. We checked out of Bates Hotel and headed out. Once we arrived at Madrid International Airport and checked our bags, it would be about one hour before boarding the plane.

We all made one final quick tour of the shops at the airport. Our flight number was called, and it was time to board. Two girls had not yet returned. Our flight number was called again. The two girls still had not returned. An envoy was sent out. Final call for our flight. The envoy returned with the missing girls, none too soon. Nancy was eating a hot dog and did not hear the announcements.

Late on the seventeenth day, the Spanish Travelers arrived back at the St. Louis International Airport. Parents arrived to pick up their children. The travelers were completely worn out and too tired to speak of their great adventures.

The Spanish Travelers survived, and so did Spain. The invasion was deemed by everyone to be a success.

At the time the trip to Spain was not one I would have deliberately made. There were many more interesting places in the world to go. Hawaii, Alaska, or Australia, for example. I am glad I went. Christopher Columbus began his voyage to our country from Spain. Spain financed his trip. Our history is definitely connected.

The Intervention
(How God is
Dealing with Me)

This book is not about religion, nor does it intend to make judgments about it. However, how I feel about God is an important chapter in my life.

Everyone has to deal with God in one way or another. It is my opinion that we all fall into one of four categories in our dealings with God. An atheist does not believe in the existence of God. An agnostic is confused. He is one who does not necessarily believe in God, but he does accept the possibility that He may exist. The third category is the person who believes in a false god. This person worships money, power, work, etc., above all else. I consider myself a Christian, so I believe the fourth category is one who believes in the Christian God.

Up until just a few years ago, actually, it was March 3, 2000, I was more of an agnostic. I am pretty sure that had a lot to do with my upbringing. I am not sure if my dad was an atheist or an agnostic. I don't ever remember him telling me what he believed in. Whenever he brought up religion, it was usually negative.

My dad's dad was Catholic, and he studied for the Catholic priesthood. He supposedly got expelled from seminary school. I honestly do not know if that was true, but that is the story I remember Dad telling me. Dad would remind me periodically that since his father married outside the church, he and his siblings were bastards (illegitimate children) in the eyes of the

Catholic Church. I do not know if that statement is true, but if my dad said it, it was a fact.

When my father first began his optometric practice, he joined and became a deacon in a local church. That church had many of the community's well-to-do as its members. He told me that being involved in church was a good business move. I was even confirmed in that church. That was the last time for many years I was in a church, except for weddings.

Because my wife is Lutheran, we got married in a Lutheran church. I started attending Lutheran church services only after we had children. I didn't particularly want to go, but I believed it to be a beneficial experience for the children. So I helped CJ drag the kids to church.

During my career with the Boy Scouts, I lived and worked in several communities. I made sure to join a church, preferably the one where the money was. That would make raising money (a major responsibility of my professional career) a little easier. I remembered that Dad said being in a church was good business.

Of great significance to the Boy Scouts is belief in God. God is included in the Scout oath. Whether I believed in God or not, it was important to, at the very least, pretend as if I did. I spent over eight years in that profession being a pretender. Deep down, I always felt a little guilty about that. I think that when it came time to leave the Boy Scouts, there was some sense of relief.

After I left the Scouts, I spent the next four years looking for full-time employment. I returned to my hometown. Once again, I joined a church that my wife chose. It didn't make any difference to me. I had been away from my hometown for about twenty-five years, and I needed some exposure. Church was a good place to do that.

My wife and I became very active in church activities and became members of various boards. I taught Sunday school to seventh and eighth graders. That one was tough. I actually had to study parts of the Bible. Once again, I had those guilty feelings. I was supposed to teach a bunch of church stuff to young people. I was always afraid they were going to ask me a question I couldn't answer. My secret would then be out. I got through those three years without being "outted."

That period was also spent trying to find employment that would provide a decent income for my growing family. I fortunately found that in the Department of Corrections. It is there that I began to learn about the existence of God.

In my career with corrections, so far, I have worked in three prisons. I have been a prison guard and an educator. As an educator, I worked in a prison with another educator who was responsible for starting my journey of discovery.

This educator, Terry Hanson, and I became good friends. We would spend our spare time talking and dreaming of retirement.

Terry had two goals when he retired. One was to own more rental property. He already had several, and one of them, he told me, was presenting him with a rent collection challenge. He could not get his current renters to pay. They were several months behind. The day we talked about his rental dreams he had already come up with a surefire solution to his rent collection problem. He said government regulations would not allow him to kick renters out, so he figured that since he owned the house he had an obligation to install a new burglarproof lock on the door. His catch was, he had to remove the door to take it to the installer. That meant the renters would be without a front door. He figured it would not be long before his renters would be gone. We both laughed about that. I don't really know if he actually did remove the door. He did tell me later that those renters were gone.

Terry also planned on buying a big thirty-five foot camping trailer. He was going to use that trailer to travel around the country. I told him I didn't think he could manage that because big campers were expensive. I reminded him that he would probably have to buy a big rig to attach to the front end of camper he wanted. The dollars were mounting up for his dream. We finally agreed teachers don't make that kind of money.

Terry would kid about my dream of writing a best-selling novel. I told him he should be concerned. I already had been making notes, and he would be part of it. Of course he didn't believe me. The last I heard, Terry did get a camper, downsized a bit, and has traveled the US with it.

Besides sharing our dreams, we would open up to each other about our past. I would tell him about my dominating father, and he would tell me about his alcoholic past.

In one of our talks, he told me that he found Jesus in one of his drunken stupors. Terry said he wasn't a praying man, but on that day he had had enough and could take no more. Terry said he went back behind his barn, sat down on the fence, and had a talk with Jesus. It was a typical talk. "Why me? What did I do to deserve this? If you really do exist, show me a sign." Terry said he sat on that fence for three hours talking to Jesus until he had no more to say. Then he went to bed. He woke up a changed man

I remember thinking that was a story told many times by many people. But this story was different. This was Terry. This was someone I personally knew and respected a great deal. I believed he really believed what he was telling me was true.

The prison was frequently locked down, so classes would be canceled. To help pass time, Terry and I would often walk around the gym. During one of those walks, he asked me a question that absolutely stirred my very soul. "Pete," he asked, "do you believe in Jesus?" Believe it or not, no one had ever asked me that question before. I wasn't sure of the politically correct answer. I had to think for a moment. All I could come up with was, "I don't know." Terry was not going to accept that answer.

"Do you believe in heaven and hell?" Terry asked.

Another soul-shaking question for me. This walk was now becoming very uncomfortable, and I was wishing it would come to a quick end. I thought, *Why doesn't this lockdown end right now so I can get back to class?* Dealing with criminals would be easier than dealing with this.

"I'm not sure. I'd like to believe in heaven. I think I do. As for hell, I hope it doesn't exist."

"If you believe in heaven, how do you plan to get there?"

"I am a good person. I always try to set a good example."

Terry then asked me *the* question. "Pete, if you don't believe in Jesus, then how can you get to heaven?" That question made me stop right then, right there, in my tracks. Did he just tell me I wasn't getting to heaven if I didn't believe in Jesus? Wasn't exactly sure what heaven was. I did know I wanted to get there. And Terry just told me I may not make it there. For some reason unknown to me at the time, that question made a lot of sense to me. I knew I was going to have to contemplate on it. No one had ever asked me a question like that before.

I never got the chance to thank Terry for the day's conversion. That walk, for some reason I can no longer remember, was ended. We never again had a chance to renew that conversation, and our paths have since gone in different directions. Terry retired, and I moved to a different prison to teach.

Because of that conversation, I became receptive to hearing about God. Suddenly I started hearing more and more people talk about God in my presence. I would listen and not make excuses to leave. I even read the Bible cover to cover.

One day, March 3, 2000, I was feeling very alone. I was feeling as if no one in the world liked me and didn't really care about my existence here on earth. I was about to have my Terry Hanson moment. I remember driving home from work and being ready to blame my wife for all my problems. As soon as I walked in the door, I started in on her. When she didn't accept the blame, I left her and spent the night alone in a motel. I spent most of the night blaming everyone but me. Eventually, I was able to close my eyes and sleep. God woke me up that night and spoke to me.

Terry told me once that God spoke to him. But of course, I didn't believe it. All those "so-called" Christians say that. I believe Terry now.

God was intervening in my life. There is no way I could have figured out my problem on my own. I heard him say two words to me. No, it wasn't a booming voice. It wasn't even a soft voice. Two words just came to me: *choice* and *consequences*.

Up until that day, I allowed others to tell me what to do. My father told me what he expected me to be and who my friends should be. I felt my siblings and friends expected certain things of me as well. I felt if I did not do things their way, I would be unwanted. I lived my live always wanting to be accepted. I was incapable of thinking or making decisions on my own.

Choice. To live the way I was living was my choice. No one forced me to live that way.

Consequences. All the loneliness and insecurities I felt happened because I chose to let others dictate to me.

If I don't like the way my life is going or what others are doing or saying, I have a choice. I can accept it or not and move on or not.

What happens as a result (consequence) of my choice is no one's fault but mine. Knowing that is really empowering.

What a difference those two words God gave me have made in my life. God supplied me with those words and gave me comfort. I now know he is in control.

My life is good. Where I am now is where God brought me. I am not smart enough to have planned out this path. God guided me in spite of my stupid self. I have absolutely no doubt now that the adventures I have had up to this point were because of God's plan for me. I realized at that moment that God intended me to go through all those adventures. He had a plan for me and would reveal it to me when I was ready. I remembered that Terry Hanson had told me that too. It is a great comfort to know that God is in control.

God has always been with me, guiding me, leading me, pointing me in the right direction. Until 2000, I was not aware of his presence, which is why no mention was made of him until now. Didn't acknowledge him; how could I include him in the retelling of my adventures?

I know that God will never abandon me. Whenever I believe he might, he will do something to remind me he is with me. This book is an example. I needed an outlet for many years. Here you are reading my story about how God is dealing with me.

Murder in My Classroom

A murder was committed in my classroom in my presence.

I teach GED in a prison. My classroom is full of rapists, thieves, and killers who come to see me every day. They come for various reasons. Some come to socialize. Some come to just get out of their cells and soak up the air-conditioning. And still others come to legitimately try to learn something. My job is to try to enhance their brainpower in some small way, regardless of their reason for being in my room.

As a GED teacher, I am to teach five subject areas. They are reading, math, writing, social studies, and science. In my classroom environment I have a variety of academic levels. Some of my students can barely read but understand algebra. I have others who can do geometry but cannot read.

Taking GED is voluntary. A student can be with me today and decide to quit tomorrow. The next day his seat is filled with a new student. Keeping everyone on the same page is difficult. But such is the life of an educator in an Illinois prison system.

Occasionally, I give my class the opportunity to talk about their plans when they get back out on the street. I am usually not surprised by their positive responses. I always hope what they tell me is truthful. I know sometimes I am just getting a story that sounds like something they think I want to hear.

I do remember one inmate student's response to the life after prison question. His response was, "I sold drugs to get in here. I will sell drugs when I get out. There's lots of money it." With confidence he added, "I know I make more money in one day selling drugs on the street than you make in a year trying to teach me geometry. I'd sell drugs to my son if it meant I could make the money." With an attitude like that, sometimes all I can do is my job.

Sometimes I learn from my students. Once again I had the life after prison lesson. I asked a student what he planned to do with the knowledge he was getting by being in my GED class. His response, "Street-side pharmaceuticals." What was my lesson learned? I learned a new career title.

On that fateful day, when the murder in my classroom happened, I was teaching American history. The trouble started when a bully somehow appeared in my room. He entered uninvited, unwanted, and extremely agitated. He was, without a doubt, the smallest in the room. Yet every single man in the room seemed to be terrified. Everyone knew him, what he was about, and what he was capable of doing to each man in the room. He had a reputation everyone was familiar with. No one knew why he entered. But we all knew he was there.

This bully threatened every person in the classroom (myself included). He got right in the face of almost everyone. Someone took a jab at him; he quickly outmaneuvered the jab and moved on to someone else.

My classroom is full of felons. They are all tough men. For some, fighting is all they know. When they were on the street, they might use fists, knives, guns, whatever is handy. Possibly, some of the men in my room were here for that very reason. Yet this little guy had everyone in my room terrified.

The bully charged another student. He almost fell out of his chair trying to get out of the way. A couple of the students threatened to kill the bully and took up offensive postures against him. One, with American history book in hand, even followed the bully around the room in an attempt to kill him. Some of these tough men were pleading with the bully to leave them alone. You could see the fear in their eyes. They wanted to hide. But where can you hide in a wide open classroom?

Chairs were scooting, inmates were yelling at the intruder, and me, guess what I was doing? I was being a good role model for my students. Violence was not something I was going to demonstrate or advocate. I took the nonviolent approach and used strong words of encouragement instead. I just told the students, "Leave him alone, and he will leave you alone. You will only make him more angry if you retaliate."

I kept telling the bully to leave the room. (By this time, the history lesson was in a definite holding pattern.) I was getting desperate to return to the lesson and starting to think that I would have to take stronger action.

And then it happened.

One of my students picked up a book and hit the bully, knocking him to the floor. One student yelled, "Now you've done it! You've really made him mad."

But the bully stayed on the floor and didn't get

up. Another student approached the bully and pronounced him, "Dead, dead, dead."

The bully, the pest, the wasp was murdered that day.

A Date with Brianna

Many eighteen-year-olds are eager to move out of Mom and Dad's house and live on their own. Our daughter was no different. After graduating from high school, she was ready to move out and on to tackle college life. Although her mother and I were prepared to send our daughter to a four-year college, Brianna decided to attend a local junior college. We found an apartment both parents and daughter could agree upon a few miles from the school.

This adventure involves my daughter and me a year later.

I believe, as parents, we do not always take the opportunity to tell our kids how proud we are of them and how important they are to us. I wanted and needed to tell my daughter those things. Nor do we take advantage of the opportunities for our children to demonstrate how much they have grown up. A few years earlier I would not have thought such things were important. But I am a different man now. I know how to be a better father.

I hadn't seen my daughter for two or three weeks, so I took a day off to visit her. Because of my schedule and her class schedule, we very seldom had alone time together. I usually accompanied her mother when we all visited. It was her Christmas break, so I planned to take her to lunch and do some Christmas shopping with her. I met Brianna at her apartment. We got in my car and headed for the Steak 'n Shake restaurant in Carbondale, Illinois.

The noontime crowd had already arrived. The place was packed. I don't like crowds. Never really did. In a packed restaurant it's hard to hear, and I'm always concerned that strangers would be listening in on my private conversations.

My wife told me once not to worry about it. Besides, she said, "If you worry about someone listening in on our private conversation, doesn't that mean the only way you know about that is because you're listening in on someone else's conversation?" I have to admit she's right, but that doesn't make it any easier for me to eat in a crowded restaurant.

Despite my aversions to crowds, Brianna and I had a good lunch and even better conversation. There was no talk of any former father/daughter complication. She told me how much she was enjoying school. And I believed her. My little girl was growing up. It was becoming evident I couldn't think of her as my little girl anymore.

I think the chat in Steak 'n Shake was the first time I began to think that way about my daughter.

Our lunch was finished. It was now time to pay for the food and go to the mall to do the shopping Brianna was really looking forward to.

As I walked up to the counter to pay, I pulled my billfold out. Uh-oh! I forgot to put money in it. Because I work in a prison, I'm in the habit of not carrying money in my billfold. I really was not worried, though. I had plastic. Every restaurant accepts plastic. Not so, Steak 'n Shake. As you can imagine, I had a problem.

I'm the parent. As the parent, I am to take care of my offspring.

So I ask you, what is more embarrassing to an adult? Washing dishes or asking your child for money? I definitely did not want to get my dainty hands looking like prunes. I chose the other embarrassing option.

I asked Brianna if she had her checkbook. I would pay her back. She did. Problem solved. That was easy enough. But somehow I knew I would have to pay Brianna back in more than currency. Someday, somewhere, somehow at a moment I would least enjoy, she would remind me that I owed her.

The young man behind the cash register overheard our conversation and gave us more bad news. Checks weren't accepted.

I lived over an hour away from Carbondale, and Brianna lived only about ten minutes. My daughter was showing me how grown up she had become by making an adult suggestion. I could stay as a hostage in the restaurant. She would drive my car to her apartment and get enough cash to bail me out. I was proud of her.

The cashier would have nothing to do with her suggestion. He was only interested in trying to collect the payment due from these two deadbeats. I am usually a man who understands the other point of view, but this young man was sure giving me the impression he wasn't the least bit interested in mine. All of a sudden he yelled across the restaurant. "Mr. James, these two just had lunch and don't have any money to pay for their food."

The restaurant was still filled with customers. You could hear a pin drop. Everyone in the place stopped chewing, talking, or whatever they were doing. In unison every last one of them turned their heads to the cashier. Brianna and I really knew it wasn't the cashier they were looking at. They were checking out the deadbeats at the front counter.

As quickly as they turned our direction, they turned their attention to Mr. James. I guess they wanted to watch the restaurant manager throw the bums out.

I was looking for Alan Fundt to come around the corner and say, "Smile, you're on Candid Camera."

Brianna turned beet red from embarrassment, and so was I. Mr. James, the manager, arrived to see how he could resolve the situation. I told him why I did not have any cash on me, that I did have a credit card, that we could write a check, and we most assuredly wanted to pay for our food.

Mr. James, I hoped, was an understanding man. He said the problem was that the restaurant never did accept credit cards or checks. Our timing was bad because the next day they were going to start accepting credit cards.

While the manager was talking to us, an older man with long scraggly hair, broken teeth, and badly wrinkled clothes approached the counter. Brianna and I were about to have more salt rubbed into our wounds. He offered to pay for our food. I still remember thinking, *That man looks like he can't pay his own bill. How is he going to pay for mine?* I sure didn't want to be beholden to someone who looked like a bum. I was also ashamed of myself for even thinking that of the man. I thanked the man for his kind offer and told him I was sure the manager and I could work something out.

Brianna could hardly stand it. I don't think she could have gotten any redder.

By now I had the manager sized up as a reasonable person. We were going to amicably resolve this dreadful situation. Mr. James finally said he would accept my credit card. He would let us be the first to use his new credit card machine. One day early would not matter.

We thanked Mr. James and headed for the mall only to be embarrassed again.

Brianna finished her shopping, and we headed for the car. Once again, I had a problem with my keys. Just like I had with my cousin Jake on Rebedeoux River, I locked my keys in my car. This time, I had a cell phone. It didn't do us any good, though. It was locked in the car. My daughter left hers at her apartment. We had to go back into the mall and ask mall security to call for a wrecker.

It was the middle of December, and cold, and snowing, and we were waiting outside by my car, watching as the wrecker passed by us three or four times. Finally he found us and asked how he could help. I told him what I did and asked if he could get my keys. He assured us he could. Fortunately, he accepted credit cards. A restaurant would not, but a wrecker service would.

By the way, the next evening CJ and I were watching television. A commercial came on for Steak 'n Shake. They were proudly advertising they were now accepting plastic. Talk about a day late and a dollar short. Brianna and I could have made that commercial. I gave some thought to writing them about my credit card adventure. I never did follow through.

The moral to this story is now I always carry a secret stash of cash in my billfold, and I pat myself down for keys before closing the car door.

Post Card

PLACE STAMP HERE
DOMESTIC ONE CENT
FOREIGN TWO CENTS

The Racing Zebra

FOR ADDRESS ONLY

My wife and I worked hard to ensure our children did not get everything they wanted. That practice would make life too easy for them, and as you know, life is not always easy. But sometimes best-laid plans do not work out as expected. This adventure is about an offspring obtaining a want in spite parent's attempt to the contrary.

CJ and I spent many late nights arguing with our son, Rich, about why he was not going to get a motorcycle at seventeen. We weren't buying into his arguments that his friends had them, he was working and could afford it, he knew how to take care of it, and it wasn't going to be any bother for us. Parents are all too familiar with these arguments.

But Rich got the better of us. We certainly did not see this one coming. In fact, we were quite sure we wore him out because he quit talking about it. We did not know what he knew, and he wasn't sharing his knowledge.

One day in the spring of his eighteenth year, Rich fessed up. He bought a motorcycle without our knowledge or permission. What's more, he had it hidden from us for three days. He told us we couldn't legally do anything about it because he was eighteen, and he bought it with his own money. He had the sales receipt and insurance to prove it.

There really wasn't much to do except to express our disapproval and disappointment. He was going to have to live with the consequences. We told him in no uncertain terms we were going to have nothing to do with the bike.

Still, one question had to be asked. CJ and I were pretty aware of the things our children did. Some things got by us, but not as much as they thought. So just how did Richard manage to hide it from us for three days?

Rich and the high school superintendent's son, James, were close friends. James, of course, had a motorcycle. I think we must have been aware of that. Yes, James was involved in this caper.

One more person was involved in this secret. James's dad, the school superintendent, was apparently aware that Richard bought the motorcycle and allowed the bike to be stored at his house. But in his defense, Rich told the man we knew he had the bike but had no place to store it then. We were going to get a shed for it in a couple of days. Both families got hoodwinked by a couple of teenage kids. In time, we all got over it.

Rich and his buddies went on many rides together. They were teenagers, so their rides weren't always what I would consider pleasure rides. Rich and his friends were learning to pop wheelies and ride standing on their bike seats. I guess Rich was the biggest thrill seeker of the group because when he eventually moved to the Chicago area he took up a new hobby: motorcycle road racing.

One day when we went to see him in Chicago, our son invited us to watch him race. I was looking forward to watching him race. CJ was extremely apprehensive. She didn't want to see her baby boy crash and burn. It was difficult to get her to that first race.

Rich had joined a racing team called Up Front Racing. The team raced only 125cc bikes. They were awesome little bikes. They could reach speeds well over one hundred miles per hour and were extremely durable. I saw these bikes crash hard and get back out on the track in short order. These bikes had only one purpose in life, and that was to road race.

The day we saw our son race was probably his third or fourth race. He had a terrific start. In fact, he was leading the field. The announcer kept calling his name, so we were pretty excited. As the racers were entering the last turn, Richard was still leading. As you would expect, CJ and I were having a difficult time containing our excitement. Our son was going to win this race. And he was going to come out of it unhurt. "See, CJ. It's not so bad."

We watched as he entered the final turn. We saw a cloud of smoke at the far end of the track. Too bad, some rider crashed. CJ and I could not wait to congratulate our son. The riders crossed the finish line. Where was Richard? In our excitement, did we miss him? Why didn't we hear the announcer give his name?

CJ and I watched the racers bring their bikes back to the pit area. Where was Richard? And then we heard his voice behind us. His bike wasn't with him. What happened to his bike? We were just about to congratulate him on his win when he asked us if we saw that cloud of smoke.

We told him we had and asked if the rider was okay. Rich said the rider was and we were looking at him.

That was kind of a frightening moment. Our son had to be going nearly a hundred miles per hour when he crashed. He could have been killed or at least severely maimed for life. But he was standing in front of us with a big smile on his face. He saw the whole episode very differently than we did. What he saw was that he was leading his first race and would have won it except for one stupid mistake. He would correct it the next time. There would be lots of next times.

Eventually, Rich moved back closer to us and continued his racing. But this time he created his own team, Zebra Racing Inc. It consisted of himself, his girlfriend, and me. Even his mother got involved in it. She became the money manager.

Rich wanted his team to have something unique about it. He wanted his bike to look different than anyone else's, so he painted it with black and white zebra stripes. With the unusual colors, his bike did stand out, and everyone noticed it. Consequently, he knew he had to race like he was a standout. And he did. He nearly always finished in the top two or three.

Getting involved with my son's racing was a lot of fun for me and afforded me many traveling opportunities. Rich and his mother made me an official team member and gave me a title. I was the crew chief of Zebra Racing Inc. All that really meant was that I helped him pay some of his racing expenses, and that gave me the right to travel around the country with him. I got to watch my son mature and grow into a man.

Racers tend to travel in packs and have one common thought. If you are not talking motorcycles, you are not heard. I know very little about motors of any kind, so having intelligent conversations with these racers was next to impossible. Didn't really matter to me. I live in southern Illinois, and I could be performing racing duties in Wisconsin with my son.

Rich and I spent a couple of years on the racing circuit and had many experiences together. There is one particular experience that will always stand out to me.

No parent wants to watch his or her child get hurt. Yet there I was watching my son race around a track at speeds reaching well over one hundred miles per hour. I watched him lean his zebra-striped bike way over on its side, dragging his knee on the track. I watched him race side by side with other racers as they fought for position going into a curve. At any moment something horrible could happen. I had seen other racers crash and be driven away in an ambulance. My son had even told me of a couple of racers who were so severely injured that racing or working for them would never happen again. His mother and I were and are proud of his racing prowess, but that dreaded thought is always around when he is racing.

CJ and I decided that one of the best things we could do for our own peace of mind was for me to take an active part in his racing. He was going to do it with or without us anyway. My job was to plan the race expenses, make sleeping arrangements, help pack the racing gear, and help drive. While at the track I was to be the gofer, ensure he got proper nourishment, and keep Mom informed. That made me happy; I was going to travel and spend time with my son.

Then one day what we dreaded most happened.

I watched my son crash his bike at high speed. He miscalculated a turn, causing his front wheel to wobble. He lost control of it. Rich and the zebra parted company. Both of them hit the concrete wall hard. I watched as Rich momentarily laid on the track as other racers passed him by. I know it was only a heartbeat, but it seemed much longer before he picked himself up off the track, gathered up his bike, and exited the track.

He was visibly shaken, although he never admitted it. As a team member, I was concerned about his ability to continue racing and the condition of his bike. As his father, I was terrified. I did not know how he could walk away from that and have a normal life.

He managed to repair his bike and went racing the next day.

It was several more races later before he admitted how shaken he really was. He had lost a part of his racing edge. Richard had to dig down deep in his mountain of courage to finish the season.

I saw a lot of this beautiful country by being involved with my son and his zebra motorcycle. The time I spent with him was invaluable. A stronger bond was formed between the two of us. And I think we developed a respect for each other that perhaps was not there before.

Rich and his zebra now race in Europe. They are both doing well.

Post Card

The Little Zebra

FOR ADDRESS ONLY

My son, Rich, lived and worked in the Chicago area for a few years. It was there that he took up his all-consuming hobby of motorcycle road racing. Racing is an expensive endeavor. Fortunately, he landed a job that afforded him the opportunity to pursue his hobby. While in Chicago, he became a member of a racing team. After two years of racing with them, Rich decided it was time to venture out on his own, so he created his own team, Zebra Racing Inc.

The sneaky guy maneuvered his parents into his plans. CJ, somewhat reluctantly, became an integral part of Zebra Racing Inc. I joined with CJ's blessing and without hesitation. The traveling required by Zebra Racing was a definite plus to me.

But this adventure is not about Rich and his racing. This one is about a small motor scooter that entered our lives and the part it played in it.

Rich stored his race bike, trailer, and other racing equipment at our home. He and his mom made me an official pit crew member of his team.

Each had their own reason. Rich needed a gofer at the track so he would have more time to prepare for each race. He also figured out that having me on the team meant more financial resources for Zebra Racing. CJ's reason was to watch over her son. I could do that while I pitted for him at the races.

Soon after the racing started, it became apparent another piece of equipment would make our racing day easier. Zebra Racing always seemed to pit far away from the fuel and tire stands. These are two essential items needed for a successful season. Since I was the gofer, my job was to walk to wherever they were located and obtain the necessary items. That cost valuable time and a considerable amount of my energy. The team manager, Rich, made an executive decision.

The day before leaving for a race in Michigan, Rich unloaded a 1985 Honda Passport motor scooter from his truck. He bought it for a reasonable price, and it was now the pit bike. It was going to do the mule work.

My job was to use it to get the things we needed for the race. A major problem immediately arose. I did not know how to ride one of those things. I had no experience with shifting. Rich expected me to use it the next day at the track. That didn't happen. I'm a slow learner. The next race was in about two weeks. Hopefully, I could learn before then.

I drove that scooter all around town for two weeks learning to shift. I learned well enough to be functional.

Rich's race bike was zebra striped. It always got lots of attention whenever it was unloaded from the trailer. The decision was made to give the scooter the same colors but with a subtle difference. Rich and his mother found zebra-striped fur. They spent several late nights covering the scooter with it. They did an awesome job. The scooter got even more attention than the painted zebra-striped race bike. The fur made the Little Zebra soft to the touch. That added to its appeal.

Even though the Little Zebra was an old machine, we apparently elevated it to celebrity status when it was given a new skin. It performed without complaints. Its celebrity status, though, made it difficult for us to continue to ask it to do its regular assigned duties. The attention it brought caused too much distraction. Racing, after all, was why we were at any racetrack.

There were always families at every race. With families came children. The Little Zebra was especially appealing to the young kids. Small children and sometimes adults would come by our pit and give the Little Zebra a pat or rub its skin. Having a cluster of people around the pit was a definite distraction. It got to the point that we had to lock the Little Zebra up in the trailer and only bring it out when we needed it. The team made the decision to remove it from the team. Again, no complaints from the Little Zebra.

Little Zebra was now free to do the job it was originally designed to do. The 80cc Honda Passport motor scooter was now a people transporter. I began riding it evenings after work and on weekends I was not racing with my son. I was becoming very attached to the Little Zebra. He was my new little buddy.

I started riding the scooter on roads just outside of town. Because he was capable of only reaching a top speed of forty-five miles per hour, I rode only on little-used roads.

A whole new world had just been opened up to me.

Before the Little Zebra, I had no opportunity to experience the freedom that riding on two wheels provided. For me, it was liberating. I started making plans to get another two wheeler that would allow me access to more roads.

First, I needed to learn to ride with more confidence. Little Zebra performed that function well. I rode him all over town. I doubt if there was a street the two of us were not on. I live in a small town, so everyone knew us. Kids would wave, and adults would smile.

Brittany, the daughter of one of our friends, would come with her mother to visit us two or three times a week during the summers. Brittany was eight and enjoyed being in the spotlight. Little Zebra certainly did his part to have the spotlight shine on her.

Whenever she would come we would go riding, with her mother's approval of course. She would hop on Little Zebra's back, and off we would go. Brittany liked being seen with Little Zebra. We would ride around several streets and always through her neighborhood where she would wave and smile at her friends. Frequently we would stop at the Dairy Queen and enjoy an ice cream cone before going back to her mother. Little Zebra would get a few pats while we were there. Brittany would tell everyone how much fun she was having. I know she enjoyed being associated with Little Zebra.

Early one morning, perhaps one o'clock, the wife and I were awakened by a knock at the door. This is never good. Those kinds of knocks always generate negative scenarios in the sleepy brain.

When we opened the door, we were greeted by a police officer. Another bad sign. He asked us if we still had our zebra scooter. I told him we did. I parked it on the back porch last night. The officer said he had seen one like mine a short time ago, so I better check. Sure enough, Little Zebra was not where I left him.

The officer told us that he had personally seen two young men riding on it a few minutes before. He chased after them, but they got away. The officer did retrieve the Little Zebra. He told me I could pick it up the next day at the police station. I did, and I was grateful to the police. The Little Zebra was undamaged. What a sturdy little steed he was!

I learned my lesson. Little Zebra was going to have more protection from now on. I would tuck him away safe and sound in our shed at the end of every ride.

CJ called me a couple months later at work and told me I needed to stop by the police station. I had to fill out a police report. Little Zebra had been stolen again. This time, his life was over. He was in pieces. Someone broke the lock, removed Little Zebra from the shed, rode him away, and discarded him in the woods when their fun ended. As far as I know, the culprits were never found.

Unbeknownst to us, Little Zebra had one more good deed to perform for us. A claim was made to the insurance company. They valued the scooter's life at twice Rich's initial monetary expenditure.

I thought my son unwisely spent 350 dollars for that fifteen-year-old motor scooter. I was wrong. The Little Zebra performed much better than anyone expected. He served us well. No one was ever going to ride him again. Little Zebra was going to that big scrapyard in the sky with a job well done.

The Adult Way

I know it may sound a little crazy, but when Little Zebra went on to the scrapyard in the sky, a void was left in my life. I got hooked on the freedom of two-wheeled riding. I had to get something with two wheels and a motor. It also had to be something that would allow me the opportunity of riding on main highways.

Most men in my redneck part of the world would go rushing to the nearest Harley Davidson motorcycle shop after being stirred by those feelings. Nothing here portrays a more macho image than a Harley. Anyone within a mile radius of you knows you are around and what you are riding. Hearing the very distinctive sounds of a Harley Davidson machine gives most men seeking that status goose bumps.

I, on the other hand, had no interest in joining that good ol' boys' club.

I was not interested in shifting gears, ear-shattering noise, the mere mass of those machines, or being associated by others as something I am not.

I am a more mellow fellow and somewhat of a loner. I believe it is difficult to be that as a Harley rider. So my problem was to find something less obnoxious than a Harley but that would give me the same liberty of the open-road riding that Harley riders experience.

My research of the two-wheeled riding experience led me to a bigger version of the Little Zebra, a maxi-scooter. With a machine like that, I could go anywhere a Harley went, almost as fast, with better gas mileage, built-in storage, and for a whole lot cheaper. Also, my neighbors would not be shaking in their homes when I left or returned from a ride.

My neighbor, Jim, backed his Harley Davidson motorcycle out of his garage every Saturday morning around 6:30 a.m. He liked to get an early start on his weekend ride. CJ and I like to sleep in on weekends. Jim's Harley rocked our house when he cranked it up, and we rolled out of bed earlier than desired.

No matter what type of two-wheeled vehicle I chose, I had one major obstacle to overcome. I would have to get a motorcycle driver's license. I had heard that the road portion of the driver's test, which I could take at the local driver's license facility, was very difficult. My son convinced me that with my inexperience it would be very probable I would not pass it. My solution was to take a motorcycle safe driver's course. After successful completion of the course, a driver's license would be issued. A member of Zebra Racing Inc., my son, decided to go through the course with me. This would be another father-son bonding opportunity.

I enrolled Rich and me and anxiously waited for the magic day to arrive. The course was to be a weekend-long event. It should be fun.

Soon after Rich and I arrived, I figured out that the course would be physically taxing but absolutely nothing I could not handle. After all, I passed the physical for the Illinois Department of Corrections. The end result would be that I could get my two-wheeler license and legally start my riding experience. I was pumped. Rich saw it as an opportunity to get a part-time job. He raced motorcycles. He ought to be able to pass this course with flying colors and audition for a job at the same time. Although he was later given the opportunity to teach the course, his job moved him to another country.

The course began by teaching participants how to do simple things like sit on a motorcycle. These motorcycles were small. They were about the size of my son's first racing bike: 150cc. But they were plenty big enough to demonstrate proper riding technique to the unskilled. After showing us the important parts of the bike—the ignition, clutch, accelerator, brakes, etc.—they allowed us to push each other across a parking lot. For an old guy like me, that was the most physically strenuous part of the entire weekend.

Eventually, we were shown how to shift and slowly ride our bikes through a course. Leaning with the bike through curves is an important ingredient of riding any motorized two-wheeler at highway speeds. That was the most difficult skill for me to master. It just didn't seem logical to lean a bike over while going around a curve. On the last day of the course, I found out just how difficult it was for me.

Just before we broke for lunch on the first day of class, one of the participants, a guy about twenty years my junior, apparently forgot which handgrip operated the clutch. He was negotiating a ninety-degree turn and accelerated his bike instead of using the clutch. The poor guy wound up crashing his bike. It fell on his leg and broke one of his leg bones. There was nothing funny about the guy's situation. His leg bone was sticking out through his skin. But we were all joking about how that could have happened when it appeared he was only going about five miles an hour and the bike was so small.

He was taken to a local hospital in an ambulance. But I was unconcerned. How in the world can anybody be so stupid as to break a bone in a motorcycle safety class?

The last activity we were to do before our driver's test was to ride our bikes through a figure eight with the entire group on the course. We were instructed to take it very slow. This was still going to be somewhat stressful, especially due to the fact that the parking lot was wet in spots. I had visions of someone else crashing and starting a domino effect. I was just hoping I was not going to be part of the domino.

I slowly negotiated the figure eight two or three times. No mishaps. The instructor told us to make one more pass. I was feeling plenty confident by now about leaning my bike into the curves, so I thought I would be able to increase the speed through the last curve.

Our brains are wonderful pieces of equipment. It is amazing how much information the brain processes in a split second. In a split second it can remind us of all necessary information, how to use it, and when to use it. With that information, we can confidently do anything. Confidence is a good thing. It generally makes one perform better.

Unfortunately, that same brain must sometimes take great pleasure in playing tricks on us. At least, that is my story, and I'm sticking to it.

On the last pass of the figure eight, leaning into the last curve and full of bravado, my brain picked that moment to play a cruel trick on me. Because of that increased confidence, I felt the need to impress my son and increased the speed of entry into the curve. Just as I did that, I remembered the guy with the broken leg being carted off in an ambulance and suddenly saw the puddle of water in the middle of the curve.

Water? What am I supposed to do if there is water on the road? I don't remember what my instructor said. That puddle just didn't suddenly appear. It had to be there on my other passes. Lean, Pete, lean. Give it some gas.

Suddenly, I saw Bill, one of the instructors who was directing traffic for us, through that curve. He was waving at me. *Why? What's he trying to say?* Suddenly, I understood. He was not waving. His arms were outstretched in front of him because he was bracing for my impact with him. I didn't want to crash into him, so I put my foot down. I guess I thought it would help in braking. Fortunately for Bill, the bike's direction changed just enough to miss him. Unfortunately for me, in my raised state of excitement, I failed to back off the throttle and brake. Believe it or not, I was determined to make that curve. I was just going to complete it behind Bill and get back in line.

My bike had other ideas. There is a theory in science somewhere out there that says for every action there is an equal and opposite reaction.

When I put my foot to the ground to stop the bike, I pushed the ground so hard that the bike went in the other direction. Once I pushed, I put my foot back on the peg and now had to lean my body back toward the direction I wanted the bike to go. I leaned way too far. For some reason, my foot remained on the peg. The handlebars were nearly on the ground, so I stuck my hand out to try to push the bike back up. I did not want to embarrass myself by crashing. I wanted to show everyone how good I was by saving the bike. Can you believe the brain thinks all of this stuff up in times of stress?

Needless to say, I did not manage to allow my hand to push back with an effort stronger than the bike. The bike and I both slid on our sides across the parking lot for a few feet. Hoping no one saw me, I picked up my bike, sat back on it, waved off Bill's obvious concerns for my health, and rode it through the rest of the course.

Almost everyone saw me crash. No one was impressed with my attempted save. I made the mistake of telling Rich that I was trying to impress him with how quickly I mastered riding a motorcycle. He reminded me that I was the father. I didn't need to impress him. He was already impressed with me. With that, we went to lunch.

During lunch I noticed that I was having a difficult time gripping my soda. I still believed I would be able to finish out the day anyway. All we had left to do that day was to take the riding exam.

By the time we got back on our bikes, I noticed that I could no longer grip the throttle. My day was done. I would not get my license. I failed my driver's education course.

Rich, of course, passed the course. He didn't need a license; he already had one. He was taking it so he could feel better about his dear ol' dad. He knew I wanted to get out there on the highway and ride. Rich wanted to do his part to ensure I could do it safely.

While driving home, I called CJ to tell her what happened. I told her why I failed the course. My hand was hurting, and I was looking to her to tell me what to do about it. I was expecting some sympathy. That's not what I got. After she determined that I was not in an emergency situation, she let both of us have it.

CJ knew that the town where we took the bike class had an emergency room in it. She wanted to know why I didn't go there instead of waiting for her to take care of it. She made me give Rich the phone, and she asked him why he didn't do the adult thing, since his dad obviously wasn't acting like one, and take me there. It was vicious. After Rich returned the phone to me, all I could say in my defense was, "I wanted Doctor Mom to look at it."

When Rich and I got home, my wife threatened to send me, by myself, to the emergency room to have the doctor check out my hand. That would be one way I could learn the adult way of dealing with things. But of course, being the good wife she is, CJ accompanied me to the emergency room. The fact that she did makes me wonder what that says about me. I prefer to believe she went to ensure the doctor would properly attend to her wonderful, loving husband since her wonderful, loving, and tremendously intelligent husband was so impaired by the pain he couldn't think straight.

The hand was broken. Apparently, one doesn't need a big heavy bike to break a bone. At least my broken bone wasn't sticking through my skin like that guy who broke his leg, and I didn't have to be carted off by an ambulance either. That was some consolation, I suppose.

At age fifty-two, failing a driver's test was a hard pill to swallow. To add insult to injury, I am still known by family and friends as the guy who broke his hand in a motorcycle safety class. I don't think they will ever let me forget it.

By the way, I retook that class a couple of years later. I slowed everything down, forgot about impressing anyone, and had no problems. I now have my license and am the proud owner of a 600cc motor scooter. In the four years since passing the test, I have logged nearly 30,000 miles on a motorized two-wheeler.

That Little Zebra will live on in the soul of my scooters for many years to come.

When I'm out riding, my wife, however, wonders if I have truly learned the adult way.

Lost

A few years ago, my son accepted a job in Sierra Vista, Arizona. Accepting the job meant he had to relocate his family. Rich asked us to help him move. CJ and I were up for the adventure. We had visited Arizona some twenty-five years prior while in the service. This would give us an opportunity to see some old sights.

The day of the move arrived, and off we went. Four days later, we were scheduled to arrive at his new location. I drove the large U-Haul truck, and Rich drove his truck and trailer.

The trip across the country was rather uneventful until we reached Roswell, New Mexico. Rich was fascinated with Area 57 and the mysteries surrounding it. He planned on working in a visit to its museum before we left. We arrived in Roswell on Halloween night. We had driven for fourteen hours before we parked our vehicles, ate supper, and went to bed.

The next morning, we discovered that the aliens had visited us. The aliens had broken into Rich's trailer and stolen his brand-new generator, toolbox, and new tires for his race bike. No damage was done to his bike or to his rented U-Haul parked next to his truck and trailer.

The police were called to the scene of our alien abduction. Naturally, when a dramatic event such as our abduction happens, time does not move quickly enough. We wanted this whole affair put behind us so we could move on with our lives. It seemed like it took hours for the police to arrive. The officer, a young blond lady about my son's age, got out of the car and walked over to us. I was concerned that her attractiveness would distract Rich from his task of explaining the abduction. To Rich's credit, it didn't.

In our elevated state of agitation, it appeared as if she was not really interested in what we had to say. We were convinced she was only there to gather facts and nothing more. I'm sure she was being very precise in her note taking, but it would not have mattered to us then. She wasn't doing enough.

The young lady took our names and license information. We were informed that our abduction was not the first to happen in Roswell. There seemed to be a group of aliens running around who took a particular interest in tools.

The officer promised the police department would investigate the abduction and get back with Rich. A report was filed, and that was that. Rich called his insurance company but told them his stuff was stolen. He was sure they wouldn't believe the alien story.

Our son lost interest in visiting the alien museum. We got in our vehicles and headed out for Arizona as fast as we could.

The trip to Arizona took CJ and me through areas we used to visit frequently when we lived in Texas so many years before. We took this opportunity to visit some of those places. Roswell was one of those places. Unlike the last time, this time was unpleasant.

There was one more place to visit before arriving in Arizona, and it was not out of our way. That stop would be White Sands National Monument. CJ and I insisted it was a must see for our son and his wife.

When Rich was about two or three, we visited the park with our dog, Brandy.

Brandy, like our son, was just a pup at the time. She wasn't very big, about five pounds. We called her our Heinz 57. She was half peek-a-po and half who knows what else.

The two of them had a blast at White Sands.

The national park is located in southeast New Mexico. It is a desert of pure white sand. The white sand is the feature, which makes it unique. Once inside the monument there is only white sand and rolling hills for as far as you can see.

When we were there last, we would take one side of a cardboard box, sit Rich on it, then push him down the hill. He thought he was sledding. Living in El Paso at the time, that was as close to sledding as he was going to get. Brandy would take out running after Rich but get stuck in the soft sand. No matter how hard she tried, she couldn't make it to the bottom of the hill. She kept getting stuck up to her belly in sand.

We pushed Rich down that hill many times. Brandy kept trying but couldn't make it. Once, Rich sat down on the sands and started digging a whole. Brandy started sniffing near him and stopped just above his hole and started digging, throwing the sand from her hole backward into the hole Rich was digging. It was hilarious.

We told that story to Rich as we were driving

through the park. We stopped the car and got out, maybe even where we were years earlier. I wanted to try to sled down the hill, but we didn't have any boxes to spare. Rich sat down at the bottom of the hill and started digging in the sand.

I couldn't help myself. I positioned myself a little above him, bent over, and started digging in the sand, throwing my sand into his hole. As before, the scene was hilarious.

After our experience in Roswell, we needed some laughter.

We all wanted to stay longer, but unfortunately, we still had a long drive, so CJ and I once again said good-bye to the white sand, loaded up our vehicles, and moved on toward our final destination.

Next stop, Sierra Vista…

We arrived there the next day and unloaded all his stuff into a storage facility. It was to stay there until Rich and his wife found a place to live. The motel room where they were staying was to be the temporary residence.

Our job was done now, so we could relax. There were more things to see.

Rich found out that an international motorcycle show was going to be held in Phoenix, and he wanted us to attend it with him. Once again, we agreed. It was not going to be a problem because we were to fly back home out of Phoenix anyway.

The four of us would drive to Phoenix and rent a hotel room that night before going to the show.

Rich, being a motorcycle connoisseur, absolutely

loved the show. CJ and I enjoyed it, but we were tired and ready to get back to our home in Illinois. We all left the show at about 10:00 p.m. All we had to do was get in our rental car and go back to our rooms.

The parking lot was huge, and we couldn't exactly remember where we parked the car. Rich thought he knew, so he separated from us and headed for the car. CJ and Rich's wife and I stayed together. I think I felt as if I should ensure they wouldn't get lost.

I was walking a little behind them to ensure their safety. I thought I heard Rich behind me and turned around to talk to him. It wasn't my son. When I turned back around to check on my two girls, I was suddenly alone.

No one answered when I called their names. Thoughts of Madrid suddenly crept into my brain. This time I was lost in Phoenix.

I had my camera with me again, but I left the cell phone in my hotel room. This time, I thought the camera would be more useful. Being pitch dark, all I had to do was take pictures of the darkness and they would see the flash in the night sky. I must have taken ten pictures of the dark night sky. Surely someone would see the flash and wonder what was happening. The plan wasn't working.

I developed plan B right then. I would walk to a streetlight near where I thought the car was, and they would drive by and save me. This plan worked to a tee.

Apparently, the girls knew I was behind them and thought I would follow them when they slid between some cars. They forgot to account for me being distracted. They should have been paying more attention to their surroundings. They should have known we were to stay together. They should have known I would have used the flash of my camera as a distress beacon. None of this was my fault. I, of course, got chastised for getting lost and for not having my cell phone. They will not let me forget about being lost in Phoenix.

The lesson learned here is to not count on others paying attention to their surroundings when I am with them. I now carry a secret stash of money in my billfold, pat myself down for my car keys before locking the car, and always have my cell phone with me.

I have no trouble creating my own adventures. Why should I rely on others to create them for me? Maybe I wouldn't have had all these adventures.

Shh! Don't tell anybody, but it was those adventures that made my life extraordinary. Maybe a few more are forthcoming.

Post Card

PLACE STAMP HERE
DOMESTIC ONE CENT
FOREIGN TWO CENTS

Mini Adventures

FOR ADDRESS ONLY

In this journal of adventures, I have told you about bringing my three children into this world. And for my wife and me, fortunately, they have provided us with an uncommon amount of joy. They were and still are a blessing, entertaining, amusing, and challenging. It is fun to see all the blood, sweat, and tears my wife and I invested into them actually pay off. It's kind of like investing in the stock market. When we are old and feeble, CJ and I can draw on our stocks and have them take care of us.

Children, for your information, that means we expect you to feed us, clothe us, bathe us, house us, cherish us, and all the other parental duties we did for you without monetary payment. I guess Mom and I forgot to tell you about collecting the returns on our stock market investments. You have children of your own now, so you will understand.

Throughout my nearly sixty years on this planet, I have birthed many babies. Now, wait a minute. It's not what you think. I have had only three human babies. I have birthed three very different careers, three children, and to date, two grandchildren. No wonder I refer to this book as a series of therapy sessions.

I have given you insight into three of my careers and my children. To make the entries into my journal up to date, I have to include the births of this book and my two grandchildren. I was having this set of triplets all at the same time. Life around the Russey house during this period was quite interesting.

Like most grandparents, we were looking forward to the days when we could take our grandchildren for high-energy activities, feed them sugar, in secret give them things Mommy and Daddy didn't want them to have, then send them home and just smile when the parents had to deal with hyperactive children. The added pleasure was going to be the opportunity to tell them both about paybacks.

But Rich and Brianna have very active lives with their spouses. Although they never actually told us, CJ and I were convinced children were not going to be part of their lifestyles. Like it or not, we would have to deal with living without grandchildren. There was no sense planning a trip to Disneyland with grandchildren. I had never been there, and I was looking forward to it.

One day, my son left a message on the answering machine to call him as soon as possible.

It is not a good sign when a son, who lives on another continent, leaves a message and asks to call ASAP. My son, who enjoys a good practical joke, was, unbeknownst to us, about to pull one over on his mom and dad.

Calling overseas, for us, is always a traumatic experience. When he finally answered the phone, he didn't want to talk on it. Instead, he told us to get on the webcam. He wanted to be able to see us. Why do people think the worst in situations like this?

When finally connected, Rich and his wife were sitting on their couch with a serious look on their faces. CJ and I knew we were about to be hit with bad news.

Probably our son, who was just moved to Germany by his company, was about to lose his job.

Rich finally broke the silence. "We wanted to"—a smile appeared on both their faces—"say hi to Grandma and Grandpa."

CJ and I were confused. Why would they be saying hi to CJ's parents, Rich's grandparents? I knew they could see our confusion. They kept smiling. Why?

The great news finally sunk in. We were the grandparents. The trip to Disneyland was back on. Smiles were now permanently plastered to our faces.

About four months later, Brianna called and told us that she wanted to talk to us. She was bringing her husband to our house with her for dinner.

They were in the beginning stages of remodeling their newly purchased home. Could it be that they were going to hit us up for a loan or something worse? Once again, why does the brain insist on thinking something negative is about to happen in situations like this?

When they arrived, we were told to sit down. There was that serious look again. I know we were both hoping they were going to tell us they were expecting, but we suspected we were about to be introduced to something unpleasant.

Surprise! My wife and I would now be able to take two grandchildren to Disneyland. That grandparent smile got broader.

The spoiling of grandchildren could now commence. Boy, are our kids going to find out about paybacks. This was going to be fun.

It's awesome to revisit your child's birth through the eyes of your children.

Remember, I said I was experiencing three births all at the same time. The third birth is this book.

While encouraging my children, I found myself needing to have myself noticed. Those words I wanted to say from a long time ago were finding their way to the front of my brain. They would not go away. For peace of mind, my personal therapy sessions had to begin.

Like my children, I was expecting a baby. As you know, men cannot actually have babies. Fortunately, we are not physically structured for such an achievement. I was going to birth a book.

Putting words on paper for the first time that others may read is both excruciating and exhilarating. I am sure first-time mothers can identify.

The great comedian Bill Cosby did a comedy skit about this kind of feeling. He was comparing a young man's dating experience to childbirth.

Mr. Cosby wanted us to understand that birthing a baby was painful. He went on to explain what it was like for a boy to take his date to the movies, work up the nerve to place his arm on the back of the girl's chair, and, out of fear, leave it there for the entire length of the movie. The pain shooting through the boy's arm would be excruciating. When the girl discovers the arm is around her and does not encourage the boy to take it away, imagine the thrill the boy is getting through all that discomfort. Both situations are painful and exhilarating.

I think that describes me trying to give birth to this book of adventures.

Epilogue
(A Love Story)

I do not consider myself a man of great talent, great aptitude, great anything. I am just an ordinary individual. I have been fortunate, though, to experience uncommon love. That love has sustained me and brought me through some awfully difficult times. Today, my life is very comfortable because of the examples of the strong love I have witnessed and been fortunate enough to have received.

My mother and father were the first example of uncommon love. Mom and Dad were husband and wife for fifty-five years. They raised five children through hard times and easier times. They were each other's best friends. When my mother died, three months to the day, my father died. Five children were not able to break through the bond that tied them together.

I have to include my in-laws as examples of uncommon love. Comedians frequently include in-laws in their book of jokes. My in-laws are not the examples used by comedians. They have been married for nearly sixty years and are still going strong. My wife's parents, like mine, epitomize the strength of a strong marriage.

My wife is amazing. I can't believe she put up with me all these years. She never gave up on me, even after I insisted all my problems were her fault. While putting up with me, my insecurities, and my adventures, she still managed to raise two wonderful kids. She is one mighty strong woman.

The greatest of these is the love God has shown me. In spite of my stupid self, he kept me on the right road. Without his hand on my shoulder, this journey to becoming a better person would not have happened. I am not smart enough to have planned these common man adventures on my own.

My life has certainly been full. How was I to know what forty years of adventures would provide to this common man from southern Illinois?

My only regret is that I didn't find Jesus sooner. The people around me would have been affected more positively. On the other hand, God was ultimately in control, and my adventures were of his planning.

A new set of adventures is about to begin. Stay tuned. My grandchildren have arrived.